Ulae

Ulae

Linda Lorraine

GSH

ISBN:978-1-956736-31-1(Paperback Edition)
ISBN:978-1-956736-32-8(Hardcover Edition)
ISBN:978-1-956736-30-4(E-book Edition)

Book Ordering Information

Phone Number: 315 288-7939 ext. 1000 or 347-901-4920
Email: info@globalsummithouse.com
Global Summit House
www.globalsummithouse.com

Printed in the United States of America

Contents

Introduction....7
Chapter 1....1
Chapter 2....8
Chapter 3....20
Chapter 4....26
Chapter 5....39
Chapter 6....46
Chapter 7....52
Chapter 8....53
Chapter 9....57
Chaper 10....61
Chapter 11....65
Chapter 12....68
Ulaes Rules....68
Chapter 13....74
Chapter 14....80
Chapter 15....83
Chapter 16....90
Chapter 17....92
Chapter 18....100
Poems By Linda Lorraine....105
- To All The Children....106
- A New Begining....107
- THE PEACOCK....108
- JOEY....110

INTRODUCTION

Unnoticed by mankind on a warm and hot summers evening, something happened that would destroy the dreams and life of two young people and change the world forever.
The young couple, Frank and wife Amber, had worked hard for ten years to start a dream and own a small part of Australia.
At last their dream became possible.
An old farm went up for sale. They had saved just enough money for the deposit.
The farm was just what they had been looking for.
A little run down but with a coat of paint and some elbow grease, they were soon able to turn their dream into reality.
But this was all to change.....
Six months after buying the property, just when they thought everything appeared to be going as planned.
Their dream became a nightmare.....

The beginning!

CHAPTER 1

The day was hot and dry. You couldn't see too the horizon as a huge, thick, red tinged cloud hung in the air.
Amber was out on the patio reading a magazine, after finishing her morning work.
Her dog, Hades a cross breed, lay besides her trying to catch a fly that had rudely landed on his bone that he had been eating.

Amber sat up on the sofa, flicked her long black hair from her face.
"Let's go for a ride, Hades", she said,
She took a bridle from a nail on the wall, threw it over her shoulder and made her way to the stables.
Her horse, Moon Star, greeted her, "Let's go for a ride Moon Star!"
Amber reached into her pocket and gave Moon Star a sugar cube.
She bridled Moon Star, hugged her horse then mounted her.
Hades waged her tail, knowing they were all going for a gallop.
They slowed to walking pace towards a dirt track with Hades following behind.

The bush around them was thick and alive with the noise of insects.
A wallaby jumps past but Hades new not to run after it.
Gum trees perfume the air and bright yellow wattle flowers covered the track.
They followed the track for a good kilometer.
Then something caught Amber's eye.
Just off the track Amber noticed a clearing, she knew was never

there before.
She jumped from her horse to investigate.
Hades begins to bark loudly.
"What's wrong?" Amber asked. She looked around and she couldn't see anything.
Hades was now at the edge of the clearing, barking as if she has seen a snake.

Hades continued to bark.
"What's wrong?" Amber asked again, looking around.
Still she could see nothing.
Hades is still barking and now growling.
Amber knelt down to have a closer look.
As she looked it appeared the edge of the clearing was moving.
Amber called Hades away and hung onto her collar.
Still watching, dog is still barking and growling, her horse now uneasy, she walked towards her.
Moon Star had never been a problem horse, so Amber could not understand why she was so edgy.
With dog and horse uneasy, Amber jumped onto Moon Star, she called Hades and they hurried home.

Back home, she was greeted by Frank. He winked at her, with his deep green eyes.
Frank held the horse as Amber dismounted.
''What's up! What's the hurry?"he asked.
"It's probably nothing", Amber replied.
"Hades and Moon Star were on edge, when we went riding.
There's a clearing off the track that was not there before, made them uneasy.
Have you noticed it at all?"she asked.
I will make us some lunch and you and I can go for a walk, see what you think", she remarks.
Amber walks the horse to the stables.

Over lunch Amber explained to Frank what she had seen, and how the animals reacted
"Could have been a fox around?"Frank remarks.
"Maybe", Amber shrugged.

After a light lunch of ham, tomatoes and cheese rolls, Frank and Amber go for a walk.
Hades didn't want to go with them.
"Not like Hades, she always wants to follow us, hope she's not sick", Frank said to Amber a bit unsure.
Hades crawled under a table on the deck, her ears back, just looking as Frank and Amber as they made their way down the track.
The afternoon warm and muggy hand in hand carrying a glass of champagne they go for a walk to see what Amber was so worried about.

When they reached the clearing Amber began to shake.
"Frank, this is bigger than when I saw it just before".
"What do you mean"? Frank asked.
"Truly, it was not this big, the clearing has become bigger", she stepped back.
Frank is standing at the edge of the clearing looking around amazed.
"Lighting" he tells her.
"No Frank, we have not had a storm for some time, and I am telling you, it has grown bigger".

Franks laughing, he was just about to walk over the clearing when a big lizard runs across and over the clearing.
The lizard jumped in the air, hissed, frothy saliva ran from its mouth.
The flesh falls from its bones, and disintegrates before their eyes.
Amber screamed hysterically.
Frank just stood in shock
Amber was still shaking, when Frank finally came out of shock, he gives her a hug.

Frank walked back to the edge of the clearing still amazed, as if not able to believe what he had just seen, he looked around, bent down and picked up a stick and threw it into the clearing.
He watches as it disintegrates before his eyes.
Frank repeated to do this, so overwhelmed by what was happening, Frank sighs, turns to Amber not knowing what to say.
What they were observing hardly seemed possible.
Yet it was happening.

"There must to be a simple explanation for this", Frank explained to Amber.
Frank tried not to look to concern as Amber was already upset.
"It's getting late. We should head home ",Frank takes Amber's hand together they head for home.
Frank tells Amber he will ring someone in the morning, to come out and have a look.
With that they head home.
Amber walked to the stable, Moon Star was there waiting for a feed.
Amber was still shaking; she takes some hay from the bin and feeds Moon Star.
"What do you think?" Moon Star I wish you could talk and tell me why you were so afraid."
Amber hugs Moon Star, gives her a kiss, and heads back to the house to find Hades.

Hades is still under the table, her nose between her feet, only her eyes looking following every move Amber is taking.
"Hades what's the matter? Are you unwell?"Amber asked.
Hades just waged her tail, still just looking at Amber with big sad eyes.
"I will get you some dinner", Amber went inside and fumbled around with a can of dog food trying to open it.
Frank came into the kitchen and he gives Amber a kiss on the neck.

Both say nothing as they take the dog food to the dog.
Hades refuses to eat, they leave her food beside her, and they give her a pat, and go back inside.
"I will take her to the vet in the morning, after I do some ringing around." said Frank, trying to connect with Amber.
Amber just nods; she had tears in her eyes.

Frank was up early next morning, Amber was still sleeping. Frank was restless, his mind racing, not sure what he should do.
Frank mounted his horse and rode down the track to check out the clearing.
He was only a short distance down the track when his horse stopped. Frank kicked the horse to go forward, but the horse refused to move.
Frank dismounts and walked forward
He didn't have to walk too far; he is confronted by the clearing, once again bigger than before.
He picked up a big log and tossed it over the clearing, in a moment it turns to dust.
Frank had never been one to worry, but now he was freaking out.
He walked back to his horse and galloped home.

By then Amber was up having coffee.
Franks on the phone to the police, "I need someone to come out to my place, something's not right at my property."
He tried to explain the situation.
The police were not helpful.
Who else could he ring?
Land care came to mind.
Finally, some help, land care would be out to take a look.

What Frank didn't know, was that the night before, there was a meteor shower.
Nothing's new as meteor showers are always happening.
This meteorite shower had rained down on many countries -

Canada, Japan, Mexico, Canada, France, England, Russia, Thailand, the USA, and many more countries.
And, unfortunately for Frank; in his own back yard in Australia.

Franks paced the floor as he waited for Land care to rock up.
At last they arrived; Frank shook their hands, and then tried to explain the situation
They wanted to see what he was talking about, so off they went.
Frank tried to explain the situation on their way.
They did not have to go far, as the clearing was now much closer.
One of the land care guys was just about to walk over the clearing.
"No" Frank bellowed! The man stopped. He looked at Frank.
"No"! Don't do that. Let me show you something".
Frank picked up a large, dead log that was on the path.
He threw it into the now big clearing .The big log turned to dust in seconds.

The land care guys were horrified at what they saw.
Seeing the big log turns to dust. They gasped in horror.
Speechless now the land care guys stepped back.
"What do you think?" Frank asked.
Speechless now, the Land Care guys take another step back.
They were not sure, they were uncertain. They look at each other, not saying a word.
"I believe this is not something we can help you with", one man told Frank.
They walked back to the edge of the clearing and took turns throwing sticks into the clearing and watched as they disintegrated.
"If you can't" help, who should I call?" Frank asked. .
They had no idea, their suggestion, someone with more authority.

Frank thanked them for coming, and saw them off. They could not go quick enough.

Frank's scratching his head, "who can help?' he asked himself.
Frank became angry and unsure of what to do now.
So, he made the decision, to ring the Army.
On the phone Frank tried explaining the situation; he was not impressed when they laughed at him and told him to see his doctor.
Also he was told they do not deal with such stupid requests.
Frank was so not impressed.

But, that afternoon, after Frank had given up, he received a call.
The army was coming out, as this wasn't the only case. Reports were coming in of strange happenings, just like Frank had explained, from other countries.
At last someone was listening.

CHAPTER 2

Three hours later the army rolled in.
They asked all kinds of questions, "When did you first notice this?"
"Did you see anything unusual?"
"What have you noticed?"
"Have you monitored the movements?"
Next, a helicopter landed on the front yard. Six Army guys filed out.
Frank was told not to tell the media.
"As if?" he thought.
By then, the clearing has moved closer, Frank and Amber were told to move out.

Amber had packed a bag, Frank wanted to stay, but was told he too had to leave.
The horses were set loose.
Frank and Amber called Hades, after, looking back at their dream home, they drove away.
Their destination was to be the local pub.
"We have to tell them what we know," Amber said to Frank.
Frank reminded her that they weren't supposed to say anything.
"Don t care! They have to know. Something's not right. Things are definitely weird, or the Army wouldn't be here.

Twenty minutes later, Frank and Amber enter the pub, everyone was watching the news on the tube.
They stood and listened, it was now on the news, and Canada was showing a clearing just like theirs

There was talk of clearings moving across the fields in Canada
Nobody had any idea what they should or shouldn't do.
Frank and Amber stayed quiet .Should they tell these people that it's also happen here?
They listened to the people's response to the news.
"It's bullshit!" one guy yell's out.
"Yeah! Could be lack of water", said his mate.
Others expressed their thoughts.

Frank called the barman over.
Frank tells him, "The Army is at my farm now, investigating a similar problem."
"You're pulling my leg", the barman said laughing.
The barman called everybody's attention.
All in the pub turn to the barman, to hear what he had to say
"Me mate here has something important to tell you all."
Everyone's head turned to Frank.

Frank was uneasy; he did not want this kind of attention.
He clears his throat, takes a sip of the beer that he had just been given, and looks around the room, all eyes are now on him, waiting, to hear what he had to say.
Frank went on to explain what he had seen, and that the Army were at his farm, investigating a problem much like what they were watching on the tube right now..

"We were told to move out, they have not told us why, but it looks terribly similar to what you are watching on the news".
"A load of bullshit" yelled another guy.
Others had their doubts; they mumbled to each other in disbelieve

"How dangerous will this be for our community? "Frank was asked.
"I don't want to panic you all, but it looks pretty dam dangerous to me," Frank replied.

"What should we do?" asked someone else.

"It's not up to me to tell you all", replied Frank.
"Maybe we should wait and see what they find out."
As they talked, they were drowned out by two Helicopters that were passing overhead.
"Army choppers!"shouts another man.
They all hurried out the pub to take a look.

As they look towards the choppers, a convoy of Army trucks rushed past.
"Bloody Hell! Haven't seen this much excitement in years", said a man, amazed.
"Frank", someone yelled. Frank turned to look at him.
It was his mate Sam, "What's going on?" he asked.
"Dropped in to see you mate."
"Wasn't allowed through the gate, has there been a murder?" he asked concerned
"No! Sam, but there is something happening that has the Army excited".
Sam's voice is high pitched, he is excited.
"Well! Let me tell you something that will blow your mind. "boast Sam.
Everyone went back in the pub, eager to hear what Sam had to say.

Everyone was quiet. They waited to hear what Sam had to say. Sam a true blue Aussie, a mouth of a drover, with no shame of what words he would use, ordered a beer, he took a mouthful, shook away his long sweaty hair from his face, and looked around the pub, everyone waited for him to tell his story.

"Fuck! You have no idea what they are doing out there. There are men in white suits prodding around."
"Fucking Army guys all over the place, dogs and gums, man this is something big."

Sam could only tell them that there was a lot of commotion going on at Franks place.
And, that soldiers were guarding the place like the house was made of gold.
They, the Army, barricaded the whole property, not letting anyone past.
"There are men in white suits roaming around, a heap of Army guys, and dogs", yelled Sam.
"Gave me the fucking creeps."Tells Sam, beer dripping from his mouth.
More families came into the pub to book a room for the night .As they had been ordered out from their homes.

All properties that surrounded Frank and Amber's farm had been evacuated.
"This is becoming extremely serious", said the barman, who owned the pub.
The crowd in the pub grew.
The chatter loud, like humming bees, everyone wanted to know what's happening.
Over the next couple of days, the pub becomes the place for the people to stay and talk things over.
Having the Army in town had everyone buzzing; they had been in town, now for a week.

More people have been evacuated, roads have been blocked off.
People were becoming quite concerned.
The News wasn't telling them much, and now a news crew was there, questioning people to find out more information.
All in town were happy to say what they knew.
A leaflet was sent out to everybody, ordering them to meet in the town hall, so, three days later at 10 am the people slowly gathered into the hall.

By 10.30 am, they were all seated; they talked amongst them-

selves, while waiting for the mayor to arrive.
The Mayor entered the hall, and there was silence.
After a clearing of his throat and having a sip of water, the Mayor thanked the people for coming.
"If I can have your attention for a moment, I would like to explain to you all, what all this excitement and worry is about. I have been told that an unknown threat, is heading our way.
They have no idea what it is at this moment, so now...."

"I have been informed by authorities, that we must evacuate this town."
There was a hum in the crowd .The Mayor waited until they settled, then continued..
"No-one will be safe if they choose to stay."
There was a mumble amongst the crowd - again.
"Silence please! I need your full attention". The Mayor waited a moment.
There was a hush in the crowd.
"Something beyond our control has put us all in danger. You need to keep your pets with you. Set your stock free, and find family or friends to stay with, outside of this town. Until this situation passes."
"The town bell will ring when this evacuation needs to happen."
"Those of you who live out of town are asked to evacuate by tomorrow."
"As you are all sensible people, you will understand. I would not ask you to do this if you were not in danger".

The people wanted to ask questions.
The Mayor answered what he could, as even he had been left in the dark.
"Once again, I will say, if you hear the town bell ring.
Without panic, you know the time has come to move out.
Move out in a reasonable manner, please do not become hostile."
The Mayor thanked everyone for their co-operation and left the

hall.
The town people in shock and still unsure what they should do in the meantime...

Unknown to others, two guys have made their way to Franks place, wanting to see for themselves what's going on?
They saw the guards at the gate, they needed to dodge the barriers, and slip through.
The moon was full, which made the sky eerily bright, so light was good.
They snuck past the guards and their dogs. They reached the edge of the noticeably, large clearing.

The men could see nothing but sand.
Frank and Amber's house was no more, just a dessert of sand.
One of the guys walked over the edge of the clearing
His mate watched in horror as his friend screamed, twitched, then disintegrate into sand.
His mate was standing in shock.
The dogs were now barking, He was found and arrested, and then taken back to the camp.
"What the fuck is going on?" he asked, still in shock.
"What just happened to me mate?" he asked still shaking.
"You were told to move out, why are you here?" the soldier enquired.
"I don't know, me and me mate just wanted to see for ourselves what was going on",
He was still in shock and shaking.
At the camp he is given a coffee and told he could not now go home.
He was told he has seen too much, and if he did go back, he would cause a panic.
Still shaking, a soldier led him to a tent and told to stay there.
A guard stood outside the tent.
They gave him more coffee, a camp bed a plate of food and left

him, wondering what the hell was going on.
Days went by, tests were carried out. Nothing appeared to work to stop the unknown spread.
A further week passed by.

Suddenly, the town bell rang out. It was now time for the town people to evacuate.
This meant that the threat had still not been resolved.
They knew by the news reports, that this situation was worldwide, and a deadly threat.

Some families had already left, but the time has come for the stayers to more on.
The police were on the highway, guide them on their way. Slowly but surely they made their way to friends or family.
As expected, there was chaos, some people tried to overtake, and some cars broke down.
Vehicles were dodging each other, as many people were stressed and panicked.
The police did the best they could to calm the panicked drivers.

Things appeared to be under control until... a semi – trailer, coming from the opposite direction, rolled and blocked the road ahead.
It was a cattle truck, loaded with live cattle, and was now lying on its side. Many cattle were dead or dying.
The cattle that did survive run around in in a daze.
This would now be a big job to clean up.
The vehicles that were heading towards the rollover were directed to take the old road around.
Whoever made this decision had made a big mistake.

The road had not been used for years. It was rough rocky and unkempt.
There were at least 40 vehicles tailing each other.
An hour into their journey, things began to turn bad.

With the fall of night approaching, the sun hanging low in the sky, they did not need any more hold ups.

A mob of kangaroos began to cross in front of them.
The convoy had to stop. They waited, as about a hundred or more frightened kangaroos in panic pounced into and around the vehicles.
Everyone was amazed at how many kangaroos there were.
Finally, they were able to move on and continue their journey.

Ten minutes later, they had to again pull up.
A large tree had fallen across the road, several men got out their vehicles. With so many hands at work they easily cleared the road.
But they were still unable to drive to far along the track, as every side had big boulders and rocky cliffs.
Big boulders were over the road.
Once again the men went to work removing the boulders, with chains and man power.

It was now darker, clouds covered the moon, people were exhausted, but they were determined.
Luckily, two of these men were forestry workers.
They had a lot of equipment in their uses.
With chainsaws and chains, they continued to clear the road.
They were soon on their way again.
Now dark, exhausted from clearing with chainsaws and chains, they once again move on.

A few kilometers into the journey, the leader of the convoy suddenly pulled up.
They were now confronted with no road ahead,
The leader of the convoy jumped out his four- wheel drive to take a closer look,
His dog followed.
His dog runs ahead of his master.
To his masters horror! His dog began to yelp. He watched as his

dog starts shaking violently, the dog now quiet, fell to the ground and disintegrated.
In shock, and unable to move, the dog's owner falls to the ground.
Others, who had witnessed this horror, rush to his side.
The news of what just happened moved down the convoy.

Two guys on motorbikes that were at the rear of the convoy, now fed up with the hold-ups.
They didn't know what had just happened went flying past.
The first motorbike flew across the clearing at high speed; he and his bike disintegrate within seconds.
His mate behind him saw what had happened, and skid sideways to avoid crossing the clearing.
He came to a halt; and was thrown from his bike. His right arm fell across the clearing.
People watched as he let out an agonizing scream. He got to his feet and staggered towards them.
They stepped back in terror, his right arm to the elbow, was gone.
Still screaming in agony, fear across his face, he called for someone to help him.

Nobody stepped forward to help, they could only watch as the rest of his arm disintegrated.
He fell unconscious to the ground, as this whatever it was, crept across his chest – and then he turned to dust.

Frank and Amber, who were two cars behind, exited their car.
"We must turn back!" Frank warned them,
"This is what we should have been moving away from; instead we have driven into it.
Whatever it is, it's moving faster than I could have imagined."

With their car headlights on high beam, people hurried forward to see what was happening.
Frank yelled, "For them to be careful!"
"So as to warn them not cross the clearing and to hang onto their

children and dogs tightly."
"Our kids are restless and hungry," someone informed Frank.
"We are all tired and hungry!" Frank replied.
"Go back to your vehicles!" he ordered.
"Is there somewhere we can turn around?" he asked, hoping someone had seen a way.

With three caravans in the front of the convoy, and nothing but rocks and boulders surrounding them, there was no way they could turn around.
"We'll have to reverse," someone said.
"It is going to take some time to reverse the caravans," he is told.
It was decided, and for safeties sake, that the women and children from the caravans should be put into the first four cars.

The caravans were to be reversed, but that didn't work.
The road was far too narrow.
The men took everything useful from the caravans and stuffed the belongings into other vehicles.
The caravan drivers squeezed into other cars.
All this had taken another frustrating hour.
Tempers rose, harsh words were exchanged, the situation was too much for some.

Frank finds a rock and places it about a meter from the clearing; he wanted to time the movement of the clearing.

The reversing of the vehicles began.
One vehicle after another slowly reversed along on the dark narrow road.
Frank went to check his rock. The clearing has moved almost to the rock.
Frank has estimated, a meter a hour.
With that calculation they would really have to get a move on.
As Frank got into his car, a noise made him turn around.
The caravans were being eaten by the clearing.

He quickly caught up to the other vehicles.

They had only moved back 600 meter in two hours.
Any more hold ups could put them in a dangerous position.
They didn't need any more interruptions.
The vehicle that had taken the woman and children, and the other cars were forced to snails' pace.

Turned out, other people were told to take the doomed road.
So, the hungry, tired, screaming kids, and frustrated parents would have to wait longer before they could come to a stop.
Word travelled down the line, from the desperate convoy.

They are meeting by the new convoy heading towards them. Nose to nose they exit there vehicles. After a brief explanation on what was going on, the new convoy were told to reverse immediately.
Everyone in the first convoy was now in panic.
Could they beat this fast -moving clearing?

The people in the cars closest to the clearing had to abandon their vehicles before the automobiles were swallowed up.
They squashed into the next closest car.
They looked at their doomed cars, to see the first car disappear.

As the procession continued, they finally picked up speed to a good momentum. Frank announced that all was clear for a comfort stop.
Now the vehicles that were heading back were holding things up.
They stopped for a rest and quick feed.
The caravans have stored a lot of food and bedding. Finally, food and water were given to the kids and all adults.
The contented kids were wrapped in blankets and placed into vehicles and they soon fell to sleep.
The adults gathered, for a much-needed discussion, about "WHAT TO DO NEXT?"
A vote to leave the vehicles, and progress by foot, was put for-

ward.
Anger reaches a point of Confusion.
No one wanted to leave their expensive cars, and trucks behind.
But they did agree that they had to look for a place where the cars could turn around.
After all, it is quicker to drive forward than it is to reverse.
Five kilometers of slow moving went well into the night, they were exhausted and tired.
The clearing had moved closer, and faster, their efforts appeared useless.
Phones were useless, so they couldn't call for help, as they were out of range of any communication.
All communication was bought about by passing any messages down, from car to car.
Finally, a place where the council bulldozers had once pushed some unwanted soil into the bush would be suitable for the vehicles to turn around.
One after another, the ecstatic drivers turned their vehicles around, and headed back the way they had originally come from.

The clearing crept closer, only a few meters away from the vehicle at the back.
The man yelled through his side window, for the others to move faster.
Next, someone was out of fuel .He desperately called out for fuel.
A guy ran to his aid, they hurried to fill the empty tank. Then continued to move on.

CHAPTER 3

Meanwhile back on the main highway the cattle and semi have been cleaned up .the high way was once again opened.

Back at Frank's farm, the Army has moved more men to the property.
Scientists were called in, one of the scientists tried to obtain a sample of the sand from the clearing.
He used a stainless steel scoop; he kept his fingers well out of the way. The scoop dissolved before his eyes, as did the robot. Many more attempts to take samples failed.
An Army helicopter flew low over the sandy clearing, suddenly his helicopter started to shutter.
And fell into the sandy clearing.
Within minutes, it turned to dust.
The scientists continue to try to gather samples, with no success.
The sandy clearing has already taken Franks farm and many others, there appeared to be no way of stopping it.

This was happening all around the world, so, a global talk was arranged.
Leaders from all over the world gathered online for a discussion of what could be done to stop the clearing from destroying everything in its path.

The global meeting with scientists, astronomers and politicians from around the world come together online.
Astronomers confirmed the fact that a meteor shower had rained down across the world.

The small fragments that hit the earth were red hot.
Those who tried to pick them up died; the fragments spread the virus that caused all the clearings.
The virus was spreading across the planet.
After many meetings, the leaders across the globe, decided the best option would be to bomb the clearings

The next day across the world, people were evacuated from the clearing areas.
A few hours later air force planes dropped bombs onto many of the clearings.
They waited an hour but found the bombs had had no effect.
If anything, it had made the clearings move faster.
Scientists exhausted their ideas .Nothing worked
People asked many questions; they were afraid and worried.
Scientists had no answers.

Evacuations were under way around the world on a continuous basis.
People were distressed; emergency transport was organized for those who had no transport.
Everything had been tried. How could they stop this virus from spreading?
Back at the convoy, things were becoming urgent.
As many vehicles had already been taken by the sand.
Exhausted, and in fear, they moved on.
Two hours later they finally reached the highway, and were greeted by Army guys patrolling the highway.
They explain their situation, and were moved on directed to the next town.

Frank and Amber had reached Brisbane. They were on their way to Mount Coo-tha.
As a friend, had offered them a place to stay nearby.
The media were waiting for their story, they surrounded Franks car.

With their farm gone and their lives shattered, they were in no mood to talk
Frank decided the best option would be to wind down his window. He gave them a brief update, and then continued the drive to their destination.

With the virus spreading across the planet.
People were asking questions afraid and worried. No one had answers for them.
On the news they could only say this could be more fretting then they had first imagined.
Evacuations continued around the world.
The Australian communities gave up faith, in their leaders, and others that were involved.
There fears becoming reality. Populations felt that there was no hope.
What would become of them? When would this stop?
Is this the beginning of the end?
Even the strong were at wits end, they too were beginning to feel there was no hope.
Religious people were rubbing it in like salt on a wound, they told people it was God's will.
"He had come back to destroy the world he had created, and only those who followed his way would go back with him to heaven."

After a few weeks of unsuccessfully trying to stop the virus from spreading, a world meeting was held in Moscow.
Together, after finding no other way, they had one more idea left....
An atomic bomb this time would be used.
The decision had been made.
Everyone on the Earth stayed close to their television and radios, hoping it would not have to come to this.

A High priest is asked to go on air to bring back some hope and faith to mankind.
A prayer was said for the world.
It was heard in all languages, for every man, woman and child to hear.

"GOD GAVE US THIS WORLD IN WHICH WE LIVE,
TO LIVE IN PEACE,
TO LIVE TOGETHER AS ONE,
YET, UNTIL TODAY WE NEVER KNEW.
FORGIVE US LORD, AS WE HAVE FAILED OUR LIBERTY YOUR LORD.
WE HAVE FAILED OUR FAITH IN YOU.
WE HAVE KILLED AND RAPED THE EARTH.
HELP US TO MAKE THE RIGHT DECISION.
WE NEED OUR WORLD, OUR EARTH.
WITHOUT IT, WE CAN NOT EXIST.
AMEN."

They observed two minutes of silence.
People around the world sensed a strange but strong feeling of peace.
Others cried and others hugged.
They realized the weapons that had been made to destroy the world would now be used to hopefully save mankind.

A speech was then said in all languages for the world to hear.
The bomb would be dropped on one of the clearings in the Australian far outback.
At exactly 8.00 p.m. Australian time.

People looked at their watches and clocks.
It was 6.00 p.m.
Two hours from the drop.
If this worked, then they would continue to drops all over the world.

The target area had long been cleared of all people, and as many animals as possible were evacuated from the danger zone.
This meant a large portion of the Australian outback would not be able to be used for years to come.

Australians were on edge, with the knowledge that this seemed to be the only hope they had left. People covered their ears and shut their eyes as they waited for the missile to be dropped.
The countdown was watched from all over the world.
Two hours on.
Slowly..... The keys were unlocked.
If this didn't work, there could be no tomorrow.

The bomber plane arrived at its destination.
Everyone was silent.
The countdown was watched from all over the world.

On command, the word was given to drop the bomb.
The bomb crashed down.
The world waited. Soon, robots were sent to look around the bombed area.

A few moments later the result came in.
No! The bomb had not stopped the clearing.
It was no use sending more of these bombs off around the world.
The unthinkable was on the minds of everyone.
Will! The nuclear bomb now has to be used?
Everyone waited.....for the answer.

Frank and Amber now in Brisbane and settled with friends and family .needed to go outside find a place to come to terms with what had happened.
They heard on the radio that an atomic missile would be used.
They drove to the top of Mt Coot-tha.
They felt empty inside, they had lost everything they had worked for.

They watched as the sun began to sink low in the sky.
Thoughts ran through their minds like water.
They had never bothered to admire the world around them to a great extent, , how nice the sun looked as it set low in the sky.
They looked at each other knowing this could be the end of their dreams.
As this could to be the last beautiful sunset they would ever see, they enjoyed it.
They sat and watched as the last glint of sunlight disappeared over the horizon.

Sitting in darkness, they waited for the atomic missile to be dropped.
They knew the missile would be seen like a bright star.
Thoughts ran through their minds, if this did work, there would be a tomorrow.
If not, where and when would it stop?
The world would be unbearable to live in. They would be forever running from the creeping virus.

As they watched and waited, they could see a brilliant light coming towards them.
Amber held Frank tight.
She looked at him with tears in her eyes, I love you was all she could say.
Frank held her tight, kissed her, “I love you too, Amber.”

Seconds felt like hours as they watched the light brighten.
They braced themselves, ready.
Suddenly the blinding light was above them.
They clung together waiting to hear or see the impact of the atomic missile.
A brilliant light flashed down upon them.
As it did, a feeling of warmth and peace washed over them.
They felt a strange sensation enter their bodies..
Expecting to die, they closed their eyes tightly.

CHAPTER 4

When they opened their eyes again, they knew the misery they had been through had ended.
They were not afraid, for if this was heaven, it was more than your imagination could possibly hope it to be.
They moved slowly and peacefully.
They seemed to drift along like spirits in a heavenly world.
Overwhelmed, their breath was taken away with joy and excitement.
As they moved slowly through a bluish white mist, they looked around at each other.
They could not believe how extremely beautiful they appeared to be.
Like Gods and Goddess, they moved slowly, they touched each other to see if they were still alive.
Soft familiar music played as they moved around.
Being so peaceful, tears appeared in Amber's eyes.
Not from fear, but total joy and happiness.
She had never in her entire life experienced such a wonderful pleasure.
They had no desire to find out where they were.
In fact, they had no negative thoughts at all.
Together, they listening and enjoying the music, overjoyed with what they were seeing around them.
With no idea how long they had been there, time didn't seem to matter anymore.

From the blue-white mist, a Godly looking man in a soft white gown drifts towards them.

They watch as he come through the mist and sat beside them.
Frank and Amber felt no fear from his presence.
For a while he just sat, not looking directly at them.
Like a friend they had known for years, and were expecting, he sat with them and listened to the music.
At first, he said nothing.
When he did, his voice was tender and caring.

"Your world is in great danger."
"My name is Ulae, I come from a planet you have not yet discovered."
"Do not be afraid, I am here to help you."
"We developed a virus as a weapon, many years ago."
"Finding that it was to destructive to use, we deposed of it into space".
"Unfortunately, for you planet Earth, the virus was pulled into your gravity."

Follow me, I will show you more."
Frank and Amber follow Ulae from the mist to a large control room.
A large window showed the planet Earth.
The Earth looked so peaceful,
It hung in the universe as a amazing ball or sphere.

Big screens lined one wall, showing broadcasts of all the nations down on Earth.
"Who are you?" Frank Asked.
"Why have you picked us to tell your story?"
Ulae replied,
"I come from a far Galaxy, one you have still yet to discover. I have been sent to help you."
"You may be too late," Frank replied.
"They are about to or have already dropped an atomic missile".

"Yes! I am aware of that. I was hoping to avoid such a move".
Amber interrupted, "Did it work? Have they stopped the virus?"
Ulae pressed a button on a screen.
He replayed the atomic missile blast for Frank and Amber.
They watch in horror as the mushroomed smoke billowed, high into the Earth's atmosphere.
"Your people are fools," "he informed Frank.
"They have not stopped the torrid, only fed it fuel, it will now move faster across your planet.
This will now destroy your world",
Ulae pressed more buttons to other screens, showing the destruction from the blast.
"What can you do to help us?" Frank asked.
Frank looked out the window at Earth, so small he thought.
Ulae did not answer his question.
"Do you know a way to stop it?" Amber asked.

Hanging in the middle of space the Earth looked so small. Frank was still looking out the window, amazed.
"Do you know a way to stop it from destroying our Earth?" Frank turned and asked Ulae.
"Why did you take us? What can we do?" asked Amber.

"We have tried to warn your planet; we have sent messages by the way of what you call crop circles."
Ulae hit another button to show the crop circles and messages they had sent.
"They have always been a mystery to us", Frank explained to Ulae.
Ulae shows Amber and Frank the latest crop circles they have sent.
"They are beautiful," Amber remarks as she watched.

"I arrived here as soon as I could, hope to warn your people of the danger of nuclear weapons.
But I have arrived too late the damage has already been done."

"I tried to tell the people on Earth of the danger involved, in using an atomic weapon. Like I have said, I am too late; the damage has already been done."
"What is the point of saving a species that only know how to destroy its wildlife and kill its people?"

Amber wants to know more about Ulae,
"What is your planet like" she asked.
Ulae is silent for a moment.

"We are peaceful people now; we have no war and have learned to live as one".
Ulae walked them back to the peaceful room of soft music and UV light, and soft mist.
He sat with them and told them stories of his world and how it has changed from war to peace.

His world, his planet, Plasmator was by far different from our Earth.
Where Ulae comes from, not like Earth, it is much bigger.
Having two suns and three moons.
They look so close that you feel like you could reach out and touch them.
The planet still has a night and day but as there two suns, night is twilight.
One night you have one moon, the next two moons.
"The suns," Ulae said "are further away than Earth's sun, but as there are two you still have the warmth just like Earth does.

He went on to tell how they had studied Earth and its population for many years, and had become aware that the people on our Earth were a too violent a race, to be given any of their knowledge.
The people on Ulaes world are peaceful.
They helped each other rather than destroy each other....

Ulae's world, they have no poor, no one dying from hunger, no suffering, or wars.
Ulae's world has only one leader.
Meaning, they have no wars for power, like on our Earth.
They have weapons, only to defend their planet, not to kill each other.
After studying our Earth, they had become aware of the use of money, how it has affected the lives of people on Earth.
"Ulae, was shocked to see that payments for work to the average person, didn't seem to rise much as time went by. Which made it hard for people to make ends meet?
Power and greed, left the average person near poverty.
It was noted that those in power, went home with a lot more than the average worker.

Leaders were fighting for greater power; to become the strongest, they want weapons, money, and are full of greed.

"If they, your race use more missiles as a weapon, the virus will grow stronger, and will creep over your planet."
There will be no way you can stop it. It's like a plague, quickly, and quietly destroying everything in its path", Ulae continued.

"We created this virus many years ago, like you, we wanted power, and control.
The virus is not like any virus you have on your Earth.
We developed the bug, finding later it was a big mistake, once used; we had no control over it.
So, the virus was locked into a capsule and fired out into the Universe to float around out of life's way.
Unfortunately, the capsule had been pulled in by your gravity, and rained down on Earth.
Our world is now a peaceful place..
It took us many Earth years to find the right way to do what has been done, to find out also what could go wrong

Like you we still work, but not for money.
We still have farming, factories, and laborers, scientists and doctors.
The young are encouraged at a very young age, to take on a job of their choice: farming laboring, doctor, scientist, builder and so on and to take on a job of their choice.
No matter what you choose to do, your work in needed.
Payment comes by way of what you need, not by using money, if you need food it is available, grown and given by the farmer.

If you need to see a doctor, you go to him or her.
Everyone works to help each other; knowledge is your own satisfaction.
By the age of twenty you must stay doing what you have chosen to do. you can't change jobs.
Once you turn fifty you are given the choice to continue your work or retire.

In my world, the women and children are the future, without them our world could not continue to function as it does.
Women are treated as Goddesses, having all the pleasures they desires.
Anyone who tries to disrupt peace is taken and sent to settle on your Earth.
We do not harm them, memories of our world are erased, and trained staff adjusts them to your Earth."

Amber interrupts Ulae, "you mean there are aliens on Earth we don't know about?"
Ulae smiled, paused for a moment, and looks at Frank.

"What I am about to tell you, may alarm you, but do not don't be afraid".
Again, Ulae smiled and looked at Amber.

Another moment of silence, Ulae reaches for Amber's hand.
"Amber," he said, he paused for a moment, and took a deep breath, and said.
"You are a star child, my child."
Amber is not sure what to think, she looks at Frank. Frank has his mouth open and tries to speak.

"Do you mean you are my father?" Amber asked, in shock.

"That is why I have chosen you", Ulae smiled.
"Yes, you are my child, gentle, kind and loving.
I had to make the choice, for you to stay with your mother, or send you to Earth to learn how the Earth people live. I watched you grow into a beautiful, unselfish young woman."

Franks was not sure what to think, still just standing with his mouth open.

Amber pulls her hand away.
Ulae opens a book of names; a hologram appears in front of them.
"This was you as a child, my daughter."
"Is ...Is that why I could never find my mother?" she asked, she was shaking, looking at Frank.

"Yes! You were adopted to a genuinely nice couple, they taught you well."

Frank managed to speak.
"So, I'm married to an alien?" he looks at Amber in horror.

"An alien is only a word they use, don't look so horrified," Ulae smiled.
Amber looked at Frank. She thought he didn't want anything to do with her now.
But Frank walked over to her, reached out his arms and hugged her tightly.

“I knew there was something different about you”, he then kissed her lovingly.

“So you’re my father in-law? My god, sorry but I am finding all this too much to take in. Where is Amber’s mother? Is she still alive?” Frank turns to Amber, maybe looking for her reaction.

Ulae showed them another hologram, this time, it was Amber’s mother.
“Can I see her?” Amber asked excitedly.
“What is her name?”she asked.
Ulae smiled at Amber, “Her name is Rebma.”

“Oh! My god, that’s Amber spelt backwards”, smiled Amber.
“Can I see her now?” she asked with excitement.

“We will arrange that soon, but at this moment we have work to do.... if you love the planet you are on.”Ulae smiled and sat down.

Frank spoke again, “We are not all killers you know.”
Most people on earth would love to see happiness; we don’t all enjoy fighting and killing each other.”

Ulae broke in, “You are enslaved by your world, if your country fights another country, and you are told you must fight”.

Frank and Amber walked to the control room; they looked out the window, at the doomed planet Earth.
So small, it’s floating in a vast wide nothingness of space.
The universe looked so big, Earth was just another ball, like a marble, so fragile, our planet Earth.

“Tell me Uale, why bother to help us? Knowing we are so violent, wouldn’t it be better to just let such a cruel world die?”asked Amber.

Ulae looked towards Amber, and sighed.
"If we were to not at least try to help you, we would be no better than your people."

As they looked out at Earth, the darkness around it suddenly filled with lights that sped towards them, like shooting stars.

"What are they?" asked Frank.

"Don't be alarmed, this is the help we have been waiting for," Ulae assures Frank.
"There must be dozens of them out there, what are they going to do?" asked Frank.
"One hundred and fifty to be exact," boasted Ulae.

The crafts hovered around, the sky now filled with flashing lights. Moments later, the crafts begin to fly in formation, until they blended with the.
Universe .like stars.
Light's flashing blue, white, red in rhythm as they flashed across the heavens.
A beautiful, unusual sight, it's amazing to watch. You could never imagine this to be possible.
Ulae gave a short command to his troops.
One after another, like shooting stars, they drop out of formation and headed towards Earth.

Down on Earth, people watched as the bright colored lights approached, flashing across the skies.
Leaders on Earth were tracking the approaching lights.
The Army was ready with missiles.
Guns, tanks, Jet fighters, all screamed the skies, in all counties on Earth..

Fear was strong, as the virus crept across the World. People across the globe, were completely panicked about these jet fighters and guns.

Planet Earth was ready for war, not with each other, but together, to fight what was heading their way from the heavens above.
It was dark in some countries, darkness made it easier to see what was coming .but other countries where it was daylight, had no idea what was coming towards them.
They watched, not knowing what to expect.
Those in night are standing outside any were they could to watch.
Others watched the news live on their Televisions and computers.

Suddenly, the bright lights stopped high above the Earth hung like big discs flashing blue, green, white and purple.
Leaders on Earth communicate with each other in all languages.
The Army was waiting for the word to fire.
Without warning and in tune with each other, the discs let out a tune, and then silence.
All on Earth held their breath.
Cars and vehicles stopped for no reason, computers and phones went crazy.
Televisions went blank.
Thank God all planes at the civilian airport had been grounded.

Army Jets began falling from the sky's pilots ejected, and parachutes opened.
Some not so lucky, they fell like stones.
All leaders on Earth now in bunkers, they watched waited for what was to come.

Ulae commandeered every broadcast, Televisions, computer, phones, etc.

"I COME FROM A DISTANT PLANET.
DO NOT FIRE YOUR WEAPONS.
WE ARE HERE TO HELP YOU.
THIS HAS BEEN OUR MISTAKE.
WE WOULD LIKE TO TRY TO UNDO WHAT HAS BEEN DONE, HOPEFULLY DESTROY THIS VIRUS FOR YOU.

WE REALISE CREATING THIS VIRUS WAS A DANGER TO ALL FORMS OF LIFE.
THE VIRUS WAS NEVER MEANT TO REACH YOUR, EARTH.
NOW IT'S OUT OF CONTROL.
I ULAE HOPE WE CAN STILL HELP EARTH....
WE, SENT THE VIRUS, LOCKED IN A CAPSULE, FAR INTO SPACE,
YOUR GRAVITATION PULLED IT IN, CAUSING IT TO RAIN DOWN AND SPREAD ACROSS YOUR GLOBE.
YOU CAN NOT STOP IT.
IF YOU USE NUCLEAR WEAPONS, THERE WILL BE NOTHING WE CAN DO TO HELP YOU.
I SHALL TALK TO YOU SOON."

A few minutes, Ulae was back.

"I AM GIVING YOU TIME TO MAKE A DECISION TO LISTEN TO ME, PLEASE TALK AND MAKE THE TIME TO LISTEN TO ME, WHAT I HAVE TO SAY.
YOU ARE AN INTELLIGENT SPECIES.
TIME IS RUNNING OUT.I WILL BE IN TOUCH AGAIN-SHORTLY."

With that Ulea closed.
The bright discs, shot off once again into the universe leaving all on Earth unsure what to expect next.

Ulae turned to Frank,
"I will send you Frank back shortly."
"You Frank, will give the leader of your country this file",Ulae handed Frank a silver file.
"In that file are many examples and many ways in which you have gone wrong and answers to many other important things."
Ulae told Frank, they have studied Earth, over many years.
"We know, if this virus was not to take the Earth, war and greed

on the Earth would end the planet anyway. You have been destroying your planet slowly, not only killing your wildlife, but also each other. We made the decision to take two of each animal, bird, and flora to breed them on our planet. Some of which are already extinct on Earth. Earth has made many mistakes, destroying plants, insects, animals for gain and vanity. Just recently, someone on Earth found a cure to treat heart patients, from the hated feared funnel web spider. You have a cure for everything. It has been up to you to use your intelligence for the good of mankind, not to destroy mankind", Ulae's voice and words were now harsh.

"Why would they listen to us?" Frank asked.
"We are just normal everyday people? What can I or my wife possibly do that even the politicians can't do."

"I will tell them to expect you, and to read the file", answered Ulae.

With that, Ulae walked Frank and Amber back to the peaceful room, waiting, sitting, smiling was Amber's mother.
"Meet your mother," smiled Ulae.
Amber stood for a moment, unsure.
She walked slowly toward her mother, tears rolled down her face, they embraced.
Her mother, the image of Amber, took her hand, she and her mother cried with happiness.
"Your job has been done child", her mother said.
"You can choose to stay on Earth or come home, of cause, Frank if he pleases, can also come with you."
Amber looked at Frank,
"We will talk about the possibility when our work is over," Frank promised.
"Amber will stay with us until your work has been done, Frank."
Ulae shook Franks hand and pulled him in for a hug.

"Trust me Ulae.I will do everything I can," he looks towards Amber
"I will see you very soon. Catch up with your mother."
With that, he walked up to Amber and kissed her with love.
Frank was led from the room by Ulae, Frank, with file in hand was escorted to a waiting craft.

CHAPTER 5

The next thing he remembered was opening his eyes and surrounded by people asking questions.
The Australian Prime Minister was waiting to see him, to ask questions.
When they met, Frank handed him the silver file,
Frank was asked many questions, not all could be answered.
"How can we trust someone from another world and put the lives of the entire planet in the hands of strangers not from this world?"
"You must trust them", Franks replied.
The Prime Minister walked from the room with the silver file.
Frank's was left sitting alone for an hour.
Someone came into the room and ordered him to follow.
He was led to a room with a bed and bathroom.
They locked the door behind him. Another person came back a short time later, with a tray of food and coffee. The man left it on the table and exited without a word.

Time ticked by, Frank sat patiently, waiting for someone to see him.
Finally, after two hours or more, the door opened, and Frank was asked to follow them to a meeting room.
The Prime Minister, two scientists, astronomers, and others of intelligence are waiting.
Frank was seated, and then more questions were asked.
Frank could only tell them what he had experienced, and that Ulae had given him the file.
He didn't tell them Amber was a star child, and Ulae's daughter.

"We are waiting for Ulae to contact us, how long do you think this is going to take?" Frank was asked.
"I have no idea; I have not been told."
"What have you been told about this virus?" Frank shifts in his chair.
"I have told you what I know?"Frank said.

"Where is your wife? Why isn't she with you?"
"She is with friends," said Frank.
"That's not true; we have been in contact with friends and family. They have not seen or heard from her."
Frank was a quick thinker and replied,
"She's with friends like I said, with the friends that want to save our planet."
"Why have they kept her?" they asked Frank.
"To make sure I delivered the file to you," replied Frank.

Someone came in with something and gave it to the Prime Minister.
Frank was asked to follow to a large computer room.
On all screens, were leaders from all nations, they all agreed that the virus would continue to spread across the Earth. And one by one they would have to evacuate their countries.

The Australian Prime Minister turned to Frank.
"Ulae has asked for a request, he wants something from us, or he will not help us."

"What request?" Asked Frank concerned.
"I know nothing about requests."
The Prime Minister nodded, bit his lip, and turned to Frank.
"We don't know yet, but if we don't agree, they will go, and we, and all nations will be left to fend for ourselves."

Frank was angry now; he was not informed about any requests. They had his wife, and now, if the leaders on Earth didn't agree to

this request, they could go taking Amber with them.
Ulae again, was on the airways.
This time only wanting to talk to the Prime Minister.
"We on Earth have investigated the matter, the only hope we have, is your help and our trust with you", the Prime Minister said.
Frank, still angry, broke in the important talk.
"I thought you wanted to help us, what is it you want? Where is my wife?"

Ulae ignored Frank's outburst and anger.
Ulae continued his speech.
"We will send you more messages Crop circles, you call them. They will appear around the world. A message in each one, with the file you have been given and the technology you have. You will understand them. It is in your hands to read and understand each one that we have sent you."
With that he is gone.

"What the fuck is he playing at? This is not a game."
Leaders around the world were overwhelmed.
Frank was taken back to his room, nothing more was said.
Before long, scientists, astronomers and people who were once called crazy for believing in crop circles were called together.
All reports past and present, about crop circles were now being investigated.
Those who had reported and studied crop circles for years were now being listened to.
Computers around the world worked overtime, looking for any information that they might have missed.
New crop circles began to appear over the world, farmers reporting on them every time that a new one occurred.

The world watched and waited for answers.
Still the virus crept across the planet, evacuations continued.

Homes had been lost, farms cities destroyed.
With no answers, no way to stop the virus, they could and only watch hope, that it may one day stop.

Scientists, who found the virus early, had taken the hot egg- like meteoroids to labs.
Why hot, the eggs could be contained, once they cooled, a whole new concept would begin.
A lab in Australia had one,
Once cooled, the egg began to open and then eat everything around it.

It gave off pollen much like a mushroom spore.
The lab workers were locked in the lab.
The pollen ate everything in sight.
The frightened lab workers called out for help.
They needed to be let out of the lab.
They couldn't control the pollen
Nobody came to their help.
The lab workers could only stand back and watch as the pollen ate through, glass, stainless steel tables, and not long before the lab workers were also taken by the pollen.

More labs around the world had done the same and now had the same problems.
The people in charge thought that they had things under control, they were told to say nothing.
But now, not only the lab containing the virus, but the building itself was being attacked. Calls came in from other labs; they reported that they too were having the same problems.
The media soon caught onto what was happening.
Panic set in, the virus moved from the labs and continued to feed on other building and, homes.

Without realizing, they, the scientists had made the threat bigger.
The scientists that had breathed the pollen became ill, symptoms

of sore throat, fatigue, shortness of breath, headaches, joint aches, coughing and sneezing.
They were taken to hospitals, their illness unsolved, they soon died.

Crop circles were now being studied, from the air and ground.
Mathematicians were trying to decode the messages.
Leaders tried to communicate with Ulae, with no reply.
At their wits end, unable to stop the virus, a message was sent into space with the hope it would reach Ulae.

"We are ready to listen to your terms. We need to know what it is you want." the message was constantly repeated into space.
They had no choice but to listen to what he wanted,
Another message was sent.
"If you do not reply within four days, we will have to use the most powerful thing that we possess - the unthinkable, the nuclear bomb."

Hours passed still no reply from Ulae.
Days later, still no word from Ulae.

Leaders come together, despairingly, with still no word from Ulae, after a discussion, their only hope now was to try the nuclear bomb ...The agreement was made.

Australia would be the first target, again, as the country is big, to be dropped 10am Australian time.
The area had already been evacuated of as many animals as possible and people.

Army was now preparing, and ready for the drop.
The airways cleared. All civilian planes still grounded.

The world now on edge and hoped the plan would work and stop the virus.

China offered one of their missiles, to be used.
The offer was accepted .The missile was immediately sent on its way to Australia, by a cargo plane.

Panic was now at a high, as the world came to believe that a war to save the planet was about to begin.

Parents clung to their children, unsure of what was to come.
They sat in front of their Televisions, waiting, hopping this nightmare would end.
Not able to focus on work, even cleaning and having fun with their children seemed a chore.
A waiting game of hope, wondering if there was going to be a tomorrow.

Families gathered together, they helped each other get through each day.
But some families were no that strong, a man in his thirty's who before this had a good job as a builder, can only now look at his wife and two children aged four and seven ,clinging to their mother.
Her crying, not knowing the outcome for her children, too much for this man, he walked into his shed, unlocked his gun safe, grabs a gun and loads it, he stops for a moment and takes a deep breath, he then walked back into his house where his wife and children are still hugging their mum, he looks his wife in the eyes, "This is the best I can do for you sweet heart", he points the gun at her. He then shoots her in the head, and does the same to his two children.
And then turns the gun to his own head and kills himself.
Many others had done the same, too many horrid stories to tell.

A church that had a gathering of hopeful people ,praying for help, were told today they were to meet their keeper, instead of wine and bread ,they were given a pill and water to take.
They were told they would all be together with God.

The preacher asked them to take the pill; they all did as he asked.
The preacher waited, until all had passed.
The preacher then took a pill himself.

Busy scientists tried to decode the messages from the crop circles, but they were baffled.
More crop circles appeared each day, but what did they mean?
Astronomers watched the sky with telescopes, and computers, experts hoped to discover something useful.
Everyone hoped that Ulae would return before it was too late.

All crop circles appeared to make no sense.
Some crop circles were so amazing, the detail and art, how do they do this?
"What do they mean? Why can" Ulae just tell us?

The sound of Army Helicopters and fighting jets could be heard day and night.
The faith in God now strong, people everywhere tuned into churches services.
They prayed for Gods help.
The priests on the Television tried their best to calm the people.
The whole world waited

On the front line, the Army waited for the command to take action.
The soldiers were unsure what to expect .Will they see their families again? Is this drop going to work?
They are unsure what to expect, will they see their families again? Is this drop going to work?

Will we be going home? Each clung to hope, faith, and family photos.
Everyone who didn't have to be in the area, had been evacuated.
The soldiers and leaders were ready for the drop of the nuclear bomb and ready to do what needed to be done.

CHAPTER 6

Meanwhile, Frank paced the floor, He had not heard from Ulae, and was left to wonder how Amber was going, and would he see Amber again? He couldn't get Amber out his mind.
He hammers on the door demanding to be let out.

Frank thought back on how they first met.
Amber worked in a lab, studied bacteria, looking for cures for cancer,
She had never wanted to talk about her family; she always appeared upset if she did.
She was twelve when she was adopted by a nice couple, they treated her well, and helped her in every way they could.

It all made sense to Frank now, as Amber always felt she was different from others but she had no idea that she had come from some were far from Earth, as Ulae had mentioned, her memory had been erased.
Frank remembered their first date,
Amber was shy, he had met her while shopping in the local mall.
Frank new the moment he saw her, that she was the one for him.
Frank didn't hesitate, he walked up to her and asked for her phone number.
He was surprised when he rang, and she answered,
Frank took her to dinner; from then on it was as if they had been together always,
They married in a small church, and moved into their home in the outback.
Their dream had only just begun.

Their home was gone now, and Amber was somewhere in the universe.
Frank could now only wait, and believe that Ulae was true to his word.

Leaders were on full alert, with no contact from Ulae, they have no other option but to use the most destructive weapon that they had.
Time ticked by, the doomsday clock was only seconds from doomsday, only hours now before the nuclear missile to be launched.

Schools were ordered to close.
All workers also ordered to go home to their families.
Only those who worked in hospitals, the police stations, and prisons staff were allowed to work.
Life on Earth was almost at a standstill.
People waited and hoped that another day would begin.
Will there be another day, will they be able to get on with their lives.
What about the children, would there be a life left for them?

Those questions stayed on the minds of every person on the earth.
Nobody could answer those questions,
They couldn't work, but now, they couldn't plan their future lives either.
Everyone was glued to computers and televisions, waiting for answers.

If the Army, leaders, and scientists couldn't do anything, Then who could?

The fun of living has stopped, no more going out for dinner, no more movie nights out. no more footy crowds, no more weddings,
No more fishing, camping, swimming, night clubbing, not even

Bar-B-Q's.
Life has stopped.
Most people stayed at home and waited answers.

Children were not in school, men were not at their jobs, women were staying home with their children.
Many people, even though they weren't allowed, snuck into church to be saved and blessed.
They needed some kind of hope and someone to believe in.

The doomsday clock was ticking, the wait was too much for some, Some took their own lives, and some tragically took the lives of their families too.
Some hid in bunkers, others boarded up their homes, too afraid to come out.
Others, shot themselves and their families.

Hospitals are overcrowded with people who had unsuccessfully tried to take their lives.
Takeaways had closed their doors, shopping centers had closed.
They had to rely on only the food they had at home.
No one is shopping, eating out, or having any kind of life fun.
Every town on Earth had become a ghost town.
Banks had closed their doors,
Nothing like this has ever happened before, War, drought, fires, not even earthquakes had pulled the earth to a halt.

People had given up the fight to live.
As, what was there to live for? and what will there be lift to live for in the future?.
There was no more politics to deal with, no more wars, but this war to worry about, no more bills to pay.
No more farmers growing crops, no more rushing about to get somewhere.
In fact, no ones doing anything but waiting.
They were hoping that someone powerful would do something

about the situation.,
But they are waited in vain, as no leader on this Earth knew what to do or say.
They too were on edge, hoping and waiting for some miracle to happen.
The only power they had left was a weapons that may destroy the world and all people that live on it.
Should they use this weapon? They believed it is worth a try.
There was no guarantee, but what else could they do? Everything has been tried, but not a thing had made a difference.

The scientists were still trying to work out the crop circles, mathematicians had been unable to make any sense of them .Night and day. The leaders on Earth, this planet, had tried to do something.
They needed to tell the people, who were waiting, sitting in there homes hoping for a breakthrough, that they had an answer.
But there was no answer, no way to stop this virus, the ones who bravely tried, were dying .
They had breathed in the pollen.
The hospitals didn't know how to help them.
The ones who had been in contact with the virus, had pneumonia, coughing, fever, anyone who had tried to help them, came down with the same sickness?
The cities were being eaten away, and farms lost,
No one wanted to talk about a future, there maybe no future.

Leaders told people who had been in contact with the virus, to help anybody who had become sick.
But people were afraid to do that, they didn't want to become sick as well.
Doctors and, nurses were wearing masks, but were reluctant, they didn't want to help the sick, they were afraid. They didn't want to unknowingly bring the virus to friends and family

People in all counties, England, Canada, China, Japan, Africa, Thailand, India Germany, France and the Netherlands, the list went on, saw more cases every day.
All people were told to are stay in their homes, they became too afraid to go out anyway..

Food became scarce, they just sat, hoping that the message on the Television would finally indicate that the danger was over.
But the Leaders couldn't reveal the real truth even if they wanted too, if they did, it would cause panic.
Even the leaders were fighting the battle to survive.

Solders that had been in close proximity to the virus, as it moved across the land, for some reason, appeared to be ok. They hadn't come down with flu symptoms.
But the workers from labs that had breathed in the pollen had become extremely ill.
Secretly, they were taken to an infectious unit and locked behind thick glass walls like prisoners.
They were not allowed contact with anyone.
Food and water were given through slots in the wall.
But it was to late for some, with no known cure, they had died.
Anyone who had been in contact with the virus and become ill was refused help, even from doctors.
Doctors had become too scared for their lives.

People locked themselves in their homes. word would get around, when someone was brave enough to open their shop be it for a very short time
Customers would take a quick dash to the shop for supplies, then dash back home. .
Most businesses had now closed there doors, hoping to open when the fear of the virus has passed.

A breakthrough was made in France, They had at last verified the code for one crop circle.

The mathematical answer had finally been worked out.
All around the world, there were new crop circles, some so amazing, with pictures of humans and animals.

Excited by the discovery, Leaders gathered together on computers and waited to hear what had been discovered.

CHAPTER 7

Meanwhile, Frank, who had been locked in a comfortable unit, asked to join them.
They let him follow them to a large room full of screens and computers.

On big screens and many smaller screens, Leaders around the world were gathered.
There was to be a meeting on screens, for leaders, within two hours.
Frank paced the room, going from screen to screen.
The message to Ulae was still being sent every 15 minute, with the hope that he would answer.

Finally, France was ready to announce what they had found out about the crop circles.
Mathematicians, scientists, and those who had been studying crop circles, were all there.
After a welcome speech, and a thank you to everyone for gathering together, they revealed what they believed the message said.
The crop circles were believed to be gateways, on the screens, they showed a picture of a tree, one half with leaves the other dead.
The message that the mathematicians have worked out was,' we have been chopping and killing the trees for our gain.
If we do not stop soon, cures for many diseases will be lost.'

CHAPTER 8

Ulae's planet called Plasmator, was unknown to people on Earth.
Meanwhile, on Plasmartor, Amber was bonding with her mother, and learnt why she had been sent to Earth.
She walked through some gardens, she was in ore with what she could see.
Plants, some from Earth, and others she has never heard of or seen.
Animals big and small, some from Earth, others that have been on Plasmator, were for their eyes only.
A white unicorn that pranced in the daisy field caught her eye.
She was overwhelmed; she believed that they were only a myth.
The unicorn came towards her, a beautiful white lady; She lowered her head for a pat.
Amber was crying with joy, she couldn't believe what she was seeing.
She stroked the unicorn.
Amber was told that there were more animals on Plasmator that have been extinct on Earth for a long time.
The dodo bird, the Tassie tiger, and so many more.
She is told that over years, they took two of every animals, birds, plants, and fish. from Earth .
She was informed, Earth had so much, but the people on Earth forgot the gift the planet was given.

And now, they only knew war, unrest, killing and greed.
Animals were being unnecessarily slaughtered for meat, fur and greed.
Birds were dying from chemical sprays, plants and trees bulldozed

for greed.
Even the people on Earth were dying, because war was more important than life.
She was told they had watched, as power became more important than people.
Planet Earth was now toxic.

They hoped her knowledge that she learnt from her Laboratory that she worked in, would make them understand that the forests have the cures, for everything.
Once the forests were gone, a cure for many things would be lost forever. ,She was sent to Earth to try make a difference.

They had come to the realisation that Amber had done what she could, and can do no more.
She was then asked if she thought the Earth is worth saving, if so, Amber answered that the Earth may be in a state of unrest, but she believed it was worth saving.

Down on Earth, leaders were still trying to work out more new codes form the varied crop circles.
More crop circles appeared every night, each one a different code.

With the virus spreading across the planet and people becoming ill, with, no cure in sight.
Something has to be done.

There was still no word yet from Ulae, time was running out, many people losing faith in Ulae,With no one working, no one able to deliver goods, things were becoming to much to bear for many folks.
Every day, nothing but more bad news , More people on Earth became uneasy.
Each code they broke, seemed to say the same thing.

“You have destroyed the planet you live on, you offer only hate,

war and destruction."
But no helpful solutions of what to do to save the planet Earth were given.

With time running out and no real answer, the dreaded bomb seemed to be the only solution.
Politicians decided to talk to their people to try to bring back some hope.

So, all people on Earth were now on edge, ready, waiting to hear what they had to say.
Glued still to the television, and full of hope for some good news, they waited.
The filling of hope lost, fear, anger, terror, tears of for good news.
They waited, uneasy,
Just as they were about to go to air, all communication was cut off.
Televisions went blank, computers blank, phones blank.
Now people are in panic, trying to call the television station, friends, and police.
They wondered why, and wanted to know why this was happening, but no phones were working, Once again, the people were stressed and panicked.
A new message had now been sent to Ulae.
"We need to hear from you now! If not within the next two hours, we will have to go ahead with using our only hope the .nuclear missile".
The message was repeated over and over, beeping through the universe, hoping Ulae would respond.
Leaders were at wits end, What does he want from us? They ask each other.
Minerals, Gold, Diamonds, maybe water?
They believed water could be it, maybe they were running out of water.

Once again Leaders are together, as computers and phones come back to life.
With the thought that water was what they wanted, the most wanted precious product Earth has, they sent out another message to Ulae.
"If it is water that you are need, we can discuss that, please respond.
They waited for a answer. But still there was no response.

CHAPTER 9

The virus was still creeping across and covering the Earth, more people died from contamination.
Didn't know what to do or were to go.
The fear of death was all they could think of.
Food all over the Earth was running low, the population not game to go outside their homes. Earthlings had become unsure of who or what to believe.
Astronomers scanned the universe, mathematicians decoded more messages from crop circles, scientists still tried to find a cure for the virus.
Leaders argued about what Ulae wanted, they knew time was running out.

Religious Leaders did their best to help their followers to stay calm.
People prayed to God that they believed in.
Broadcasters across the world tried to give some hope, they asked people not to do anything to hurt themselves or others.
But some have given up, shooting themselves and their families.
Others took pills, or smothered their children.

Cows had been left in fields, without being milked.
Crops were left to rot, chicken farmers didn't gather the eggs, chickens died from not being feed.
No bread was made, no milk, no eggs, no vegetables and no meat.
Only long- life food, like, dried food, cheese, and tin food, were available.

And if you were lucky, someone would open their shop from time to time.

Aid groups went around towns trying to help in any way they could.
They offered rice, pasta, tin food, and whatever they could find to help people.
The lines grow each day with people that needed their help and charity.
Factories that still had products gave what they could to these groups to help the people.
The Army had been called in to go to farms, to pick the crops, and then hand in many towns.
All countries were doing the same to help their people.
Milk farmers were asked to milk the cows, and then the Army would deliver the raw milk to whoever wanted it.
Some people volunteered to go to the egg farms and pack the eggs, as giving them to the people was a lot better then the eggs going to waste.
Bread was made each day by volunteers, and handed out in all towns for people to take home to family.
All over the world, the same thing was happening; people helped each other whenever they could.
No one asked for money, no one hurt each other, they just gave and helped each other.,
Doctors gave their time to help the sick people at no cost; fuel was given free for all who volunteered.
Everyone, on Earth, seemed to want to help each other in any way possible.

With Leaders on Earth were still waiting to hear from Ulae, the doomsday clock was still ticking.
Now set at 2 seconds to midnight, the waiting is becoming tense.
What ever happened next depended on Ulae's responds to the messages that Earth's Leaders had sent.

How can Ulae help?
Will he help?
Is it to late to help?

These questions were being asked by all leaders on Earth.
In 20 minutes, the missile .would be launched.
Still no response from Ulae.
Leaders paced the floor, including Frank; they waited anxiously for a reply from Ulae.
All people on Earth were glued to computers or Televisions as they waited, hoped and prayed.
Would Ulae respond, or at the worst, would the missile help?

The deadly missile was due to launch in 15 minutes.
The virus was out of control, more and more buildings, parks, towns. We're being destroyed.
Media were asked not to show the true impact, not to show the destruction.

1 second now to doomsday.

Leaders had given up on hearing from Ulae.
They questioned what to do if the one nuclear missile didn't work.
What reaction to take if it didn't work.
How will the people react if it didn't work?
How will we tell them?
What else can we do?
And, if Ulae is right and we do this, will the virus spread faster?

With still no contact from Ulae the decision to use the missile, was becoming a real possibility.
5 minutes was left before, the keys were to be unlocked, then the countdown would begin. and then the button would be pressed.
Would this work?

Everybody on Earth nervous, their hearts pounding with fear, they sat in front of televisions and computers, hoping that if the missile was used, That it would work.

Outside and on computers, astronomers watched the sky.
All Leaders on Earth now glued to their computers.
Suddenly the world is put into darkness.
All communications lost. Panic hit everyone.
Not a light worked, generators refused to work, batteries dead, the world in total darkness.
Hospitals had no power or lighting, nurses rushed around, trying to help those on the machines that keep them alive.
Outside the sky was dark, astronomers with telescopes scanned the heavens, They could see lights moving towards Earth.

Excitement for all that had been watching and waiting.
Leaders around the globe were now at their computers, shouting orders to each other, waiting for power to return.

The missile has not yet been launched, as all power and mechanical and electrical equipment had stopped working.
All across the world, lights began to appear in the sky like shooting stars.
Within moments, large sphere objects loomed in the sky above each city on Earth.
Flashing blue, white, and fluorescent green.
Those who had not locked themselves in rushed outside to see what's going on.
Fascinated by the lights, but afraid for what might happen, they clung to each other.
Large spheres hovered in the skies, a loud voice comes through loudspeakers form the spheres for all to hear.
Overwhelmed and shaking in fear, they listened.

CHAPER 10

My Name Is Ulae, We Come From A Planet Far Away, A Planet You Have Not Yet Discoverd.
We Have Are Here To Help You.
Please Go Back To Your Homes, Why We Talk To Your Leaders.
Your Power Will Be Restored Shortly, Please Turn On Your Radio, Television Or Computers, A Announcement Will Come Across Shorty".
No one hesitated, scared and in hope, they rushed like flies into their homes and waited.

Ten minutes pass.
Leaders, and the world all waited.

Like a flick of a switch, power came back on, cars were now able to move, computers and communication came back on.
All leaders rushed around turning on all computers and Phones.
They were running hot;
Everyone was trying to communicate with each other.

Everyone stopped doing what they were doing.
They gazed at their blank screens.
Screens flickered for a moment, and then Ulae appeared on all the screens, televisions, and computers.
Ulae's voice came over electronics..

"GREETINGS TO ALL ON PLANET EARTH!"
WHAT I AM ABOUT TO EXPLAIN TO YOU, WILL BE DISTURBING TO SOME.

I ULAE HAVE COME FROM A FAR PLANET, PLASMATOR.
I HAVE COME TO TRY AND HELP YOU.
YEARS HAVE PASSED BY ON YOUR PLANET EARTH, STILL YOU LEARN NOTHING.
DESTROYING YOUR PLANET, RAPING IT OF LIFE.
KILLING NOT ONLY YOUR PEOPLE BUT ALSO YOUR WILDLIFE.
CUTTING DOWN FORESTS FOR GAIN, AND GREED.
DESTROYING CURES FOR MANY DISEASES, AND CANCERS.
WE ON OUR PLANET LEARNED MANY YEARS AGO, WHAT THIS COULD DO.
WE DEVELOPED WHAT YOU CALL NANO TECHNOLOGY.
MADE FOR MINING THE MOONS.
NANO BOTS ARE TINY MICROSCOPIC ROBOTS THAT MINE AND DUPLICATE.
WE WERE MINING THREE MOONS.
THE PLAN BEING, TO MINE A MOON AND GATHER THE ORE THAT WAS MINED.
UNFORTUNATELY, THE EXPERIMENT WENT WRONG.
AFTER TWO CHRONICLES, THE NANO BOTS STARTED USING THE ORE FOR THEMSELVES.
WHAT WENT WRONG:WAS A TRANSPORTING SHIP THAT WAS TO PICK UP THE ORE,WAS EATEN BY THE NANO BOTS.
THE MOON WAS NOT USED FOR 112 CHRONICLES WHILE A CURE WAS BEING FOUND.
UNFORTUNATELY, WHILE THIS WAS HAPPENING, ON THE 72 CHRONICLES, A METEORITE HIT THE MOON AND SPREAD THE NANO PODS OUT INTO SPACE, OUR MICROSCOPIC ROBOTIC BUGS REGENERATED AND THE CAPULE CONTAINING THE VIRUSWAS PULLED IN BY YOUR EARTHS GRAVITY.
WE HAVE A CURE; WE ARE HOPING NOT TO BE TOO

LATE TO USE THE CURE.
I ULAE WILL END HERE AND NOW TALK TO YOUR LEADERS."

With that he was gone, leaving all people on Earth in shock, they still hoped that he could help.
In control rooms, screens were on, computer controllers waited in the hope of hearing from Ulae again..
Leaders now hoped that something positive could be done.
The virus still crept across the world, towns were still being eaten by the virus, like termites eating wood.
Still people were being evacuated from their homes.
With the virus still creeping across the world, towns being eaten like termites eating wood..
People being evacuate from there homes.
Farms had turned to dust, animals ran for there lives.

Church leaders prayed for a miracle.
People waited, as Ulae contacted all the leaders on Earth. .
The Leaders on Earth had no choice now but to listen to Ulae.

Ulae again appeared on their screens and computers.

I ULAE NEED YOU TO LISTEN
I WILL ONLY TELL YOU THIS ONCEI AM HERE TO HELP YOUBUT BEFORE I CAN DO SO, I NEED A AGREEMENTI AM GIVING YOU ONE EARTH WEEK TO DO THISYOU ON EARTH HAVE TO MANY LEADERS, THIS IS NOT HELPING YOUYOU HAVE ONE EARTH WEEK TO FIND A LEADER WHO CAN BE THE ONE YOU WANT TO FOLLOW.
I HAVE GIVEN YOU A FILE OF HOW WE ON MY PLANET

WORK.IF YOU HAVE NOT READ IT YET IT IS TIME TO DO SO.THIS HAS TAKEN TIME FOR US TO WORK OUT, BUT IT WORKS WELL.YOU CAN NOT CONTINUE KILLING EACH OTHER
SLAUGHTERING FOR GAIN AND POWER

With that he was gone.

CHAPTER 11

Leaders are fuming, what the hell, how are we to do this in a week?
Knowing they must tell the population on Earth, they decided to have a meeting.
Leaders on Earth argued about what they must to do.
No Leader on Earth wanted to give up their power to rule.
China thought that they should be the one, as they have so many people and so many factories in so many countries, and own so much land on the planet.
Russia believed they had the best technology.
Asia thought that they should be the leader, as they had so many paddy-fields of rice and products that the world needs.
Uk put up their hand up as they had ruled for centuries, so they think that they should be the ones now to rule the planet.
America also decided they had a right to rule, as they have technology, power, arms, so as they already rule, they want to take over.
Egypt also thought that it was time for them to rule, because they had so much money because of their oil, a rich but poor country.
Japan wanted the role to be the leader, as they were clever and could they could provide the world all that was needed. And they could show the world how things should be done.
Korea also wanted control, to be the ones to leader, but because they had done nothing but want power they had been rejected
America, Canada, Mexico, Germany, all try for the place to be the Earths leader.

As the days went by, each country argued why they should or should not be the leader,
Meanwhile, the virus continued to spread across the world.

All who had been in contact with the virus, had died.
With food and supplies running low, no one working, no money was earned, no schools were open, no farmers in the fields.
People were told to buy what they could, and use it sparingly.
Panic buying began, people filled bags and baskets with what ever they could grab.
Fighting in streets, for food and fuel.
People were told power would be cut after 6pm,as workers on power stations were in short demand.
Water and sewerage also to be cut off for short times,
With no one wanting to give up, Some banks opened for a short while.
Some shops were still trading, water and power still available. at given times.

Traders in the gift line, movie market, restaurants and fun parks earned no money, the travel industry also come to a standstill.
That was understandable, as they were ready for a missile that might to be dropped..
Many more had felt the loss, as no one is investing in anything but food and basic utilities..
A broadcast was made to all on Earth, from all leaders and for all to hear.
On all communications that were available, the broadcasting began

After an introduction, a word of hope, they told the people on Earth, that help is on its way,
And, that this horror would end, once they chose a Leader to rule the planet Earth..
They asked everyone to understand that this would not be a easy decision to make.

Those who did not agree with the outcome would be taken away and detained; their fate would be made by the new ruler.
Anger hit the people on Earth, they believed that they should have a say in this.
Voting should be for every person, to chose a Leader.
They are told they only had one week to do this
But with no time to lose, The Leaders of all countries now must vote against each over.

Without warning Ulae sends a list of what the people on Earth are to do and expect.
He does not speak. Printed notes were put up on televisions, computers about the rules and new ways of living that would exist.
As they read through the requests, most people were hopeful and willing to go along with the changes.
But owners of factories and companies were not so happy.
The list of change was not liked by many, but they had no other choice, but to accept the help from Ulae.

CHAPTER 12

Ulaes Rules

CHILDREN WILL LEARN LIFE SKILLS IN SCHOOLS.
LEARN HOW TO GROW CROPS,
BUILD, COOK, CLEAN, MAKE THINGS THAT ARE NEEDED,
ONE WEEK OF WORK, THE NEXT WEEK TO LEARN READING, WIRTING AND MATH.
THE NEXT TO BE ART, SPORT, DANCE, SONG, AND USE THERE IMAGAINTION. LEARN AND UNDERSTAND SCIENCE
THE NEXT WEEK GO THROUGH FATORIES, LEANING HOW THINGS ARE MADE.
TO LEARN ABOUT THE ENVIRONMENT AND WILD LIFE.
AND TO UNDERSTAND WERE WATER AND FOOD COMES FROM,CHICKEN MEAT ECT.
BETWEEN EACH OF THESE REQUESTS, READING, WRITING AND MATH.
CHILDREN MUST LEARN KINDNESS RESPECT FOR EACH OTHER AND ANIMALS.
BY THE AGE OF 17 EARTH YEARS THEY MUST DECIDE WHAT THE WOULD LIKE TO DO IN LIFE.
TO STAY WITH THAT CHOOSE, FOR 10 EARTH YEARS.
MONEY, TAX, TO BE NO MORE AFTER THIS TIME.

PEOPLE MUST LEAN TO GIVE AND SHARE WHAT THEY DO AND HAVE MADE OR GROWN.
WORK TO HELP EACH OTHER, WORK TO RESEVRVE FOOD AND MEDICAL HELP.
LUXURIES COME FROM EXCANGE, EXAMPLE! YOU FIX A SHED FOR SOMEONE YOUR PAY WILL BE FROM WHAT THEY OR THEIR FAMILY DO OR ARE GOOD AT.

EVERY CHILD AGED 17 TO 18 MUST GO THROUGH SOME KIND OF MILITARY
TRAINING OR WORK IN FACTORIES OR SUPPERMARKETS.UNLESS THEY ARE ILL OR DISABLED.
IF YOU NEED FOOD YOU GO TO THE SUPPERMARKET.
NEED MEAT GO TO A BUTCER.
LUXURY ITEMS WILL BE EARNED FROM GOODWILL, KINDNESS, AND HELPING THOSE IN NEED.
GOLD AND JEWELS WILL BE WORTHLESS, AS THEY GENERATE GREED.
BUT CAN BE USED FOR GIFTS, AND DECORATION.
YOUR AGED MUST BE RESPECTED AND CARED FOR.
A LOGBOOK MUST BE KEPT UP TO DATE BY EACH FAMILY OR PERSON.
AFTER EVERY 6 EARTH MONTHS A GIFT CARD WILL BE GIVEN ACCORDING TO WHAT YOU HAVE DONE OR HELPED WITH, IN THAT TIME, BY YOUR RULER..
THIS GIFT CARD CAN THEN BE USED FOR LUXURIES ,TRAVEL OR WHAT EVER PLEASES YOU.
ANY FORM OF CRUELTY,OR DISRESPECT MUST BE DELETE WITH BY POLICE.
THERE WILL BE NO SECOND CHANCE FOR PEOPLE OVER 30.
PRISONS WILL HAVE NO LUXURIES,AND PRISONERS WILL HAVE TO WORK.

ANYONE FOUND TAKING OR MAKING UNNATURAL DRUGS LIKE ICE,ECT.
MUST BE INPRISONED ,WITH NO SEACOND CHANCE.
ONLY NATURAL DRUGS LIKE MARIJUANA OR MAGIC MUSHROOMS, WILL BE GIVEN A SECOND CHANCE AS THEY HAVE HEALTH BENEFITS
ALCOHOL ,CIGARETTES,TOBACO CAN STILL BE AVALIABLE,IF USED IN
MODERATION.
YOU HAVE 1 EARTH DECADE TO MAKE THIS WORK.
IF YOU FAIL TO DO SO.
THEN I WILL DESTROY YOUR PLANET!"

This demand was left on everybody's computer and television for the next three hours. .
Leaders are furious, .How can he do this? How can we make this work?
But they had no choice but to agree.
With the virus now way out of control.
People only ventured outside their homes for food.
Pregnant woman hated the thought of bringing a new life into the world.
People prayed, and no one was sure of what would happen next.
Leaders waited again to hear from Ulae. .
What does he want? How can one man take control, of a planet?

With the Earth at a standstill, panic and disbelief among the people, ,the Leaders now must come to terms with what Ulae asked for.
They must find a World Leader fast.
But the world Leaders do not want to give up their power.
They all had their reasons to be the one to lead.

Getting nowhere they believed it was time for the people to vote, by phone, computers or a bin provided at each city.

All are asked to do this in the next two days.
Most votes started to come through by computers.
People used the bins and tables that were set up in all towns and cities.
So, all around the world the votes came in.

After two days, the votes were gathered and counted .most people agreed with the terms, they wanted a peaceful world, but there are still a few who didn't agree.
The good news was 90% agreed that this idea could work, The other 10/. were angry.

Riots between countries and people of colour began.
Black people wanted equal rights, and their land back,
Towns were burnt down, statues destroyed. ,
Historic buildings were burnt down, people out of control, riots were see all around the world.
History as we knew it about to change.

Ulae is not happy with what was happening,
Adults were fighting like children, over what? You cannot change history only learn from it. ,It was time to move on and be proud of the chance to improve, live together as one,work and live as one.
Ulae was left wondering if it was worthwhile helping this planet Earth.
Ulae unhappy with what was happening on Earth, Broke into the airways again

"AS YOU ARE UNABLE TO COME TO A DECISION WITHOUT VIOLENCE AND KILLING EACH OTHER.I WILL MAKE THE DECISION FOR YOU.WITH ALL YOU LEADERS UNABLE TO CHOOSE JUST ONE LEADER,
I WILL DO THIS FOR YOU.
I HAVE STUDIED YOUR LEADERS FOR MANY YEARS,
ALL OF YOU THINK YOU CAN BE THE ONE TO RULE,

BUT GREED AND POWER AND MONEY, ALWAYS GET,S IN THE WAY,SO, I HAVE MADE UP YOUR MINDS FOR YOU. SORRY, BUT YOU NOW HAVE NO CHOICE.

FROM THIS MOMENT ON, WITHOUT ANY OF YOU HAVING A SAY. I HAVE DECIDED THAT,
THE LEADER FOR EARTH WILL BE AUSTRALIA.
REASON BEING AUSTRALIA IS ONE COUNTRY FAR FROM MANY.

ALL COUNTRIES ON EARTH WILL HELP BUILD A EMPIRE FOR YOUR LEADER.
THOSE WHO REFUSE, WILL BE LEFT TO THE VIRUS, WITH NO HELP FROM ANYONE..

ALL OTHER LEADERS NOW SPRIPPED FROM POWER, WILL NOW BECOME YOUR SUPPORTERS,
AUSTRALIA, YOU CAN CHOOSE TO KEEP THEM, OR FIND SOMEONE NEW THAT YOU FEEL YOU COULD TRUST.
I WILL BE BACK TO HELP YOU IN THE NEXT EARTH WEEK.
IF YOU CHOOSE TO DISOBEY, I WILL DESTROY YOU ALL.

I HAVE ONE MORE REQUEST TO ASK BEFORE I HELP YOU.
THAT WILL BE REVEALED NEXT WEEK,

With that he was gone.

Leaders can not believe that Ulae chose Australia out of so many' other 'older'. countries.
Why Australia?
Leaders still in shock, but thankful that they now don't have to choose a country. .

Congratulations were given to the Australian prime minister
Australians cannot believe they are the ones Ulae chose.
Suddenly, there spirits had picked up.

Celebrations began,
The Australian leader overwhelmed with the news.
Never in his wildest dreams did he think he would be chosen..
And be given the huge responsibility, to rule the Earth.

Not everyone was happy with the decision that one Leader, was to rule the world.
How could this be a possibility?
There would be many changes.

Would it be truly possible to do this?.
But with time running out, nobody really wanted to argue, if this was the way to save life on Earth, then who are we to question?

CHAPTER 13

People started coming out of their homes, to help others.
Offering food, medical help, giving and swapping anything that they had and was needed.
Something on Earth has suddenly changed.
Instead of hiding inside waiting to die, they went outside to walk their dogs, to let children play. And just for the fun of filling free..

Others stayed inside, making bread, cooking up stews, cakes, whatever they were good at, and gave it to neighbours, friends, and people on the streets.
All around the world people were doing the same, giving and helping each other.
On computers, people sent hugs, love, and positive messages.
As the weeks passed, and the continuation of goodwill remained,, the people on Earth, come to the realization that this could work.

So, the time had come for Ulae's final request and message.
Everybody had been asked to be ready for Ulae's finale request.
Tomorrow at 2 p.m Australian time, they were to be seated and ready to listen.

The wait seemed a long one, but the Leaders wished that they could have had more time to deal with the consequences of imagined scenarios.

The next afternoon Australian time, the world was seated and waiting.
The first to cross the screens was the Australian Leader, now the

world Leader.
After welcoming everyone, He began to speak about Ulaes wishes.
"If we all go by the law, help each other, work with each other, believe and trust each other, then Ulae's rule could work".
He told the people that they have one decade to make it happen.
If not, Ulae would, without warning, destroy the Earth.

What he was asking they had no idea at this moment.
But, Ulae had asked for something else.
Hopefully, it was something they could all agree on.
People gasped, they had no idea what the new "something could be."
But hopefully it would be something that they could all agree on.

If they do agree,Ulae has made a promise to rid this virus from the planet Earth..
It is now up to the Australian Leader to agree or not agree to Ulaes request.
He thanked all the listeners, wished the Earth people, hope and a great future.
Standby for Ulae's message and request .after a long speech of hope, He ended.
As the People on Earth waited for Ulae,talk about what is expected, and how the world will recover from this, was strong in everyone's heart.
Most people believed the outcome would be good.
Yesterday, they had nothing to look forward to, maybe tomorrow would bring a new beginning.

Finally, after they waited for what seemed a long time, the clock struck 2.
Ulae appeared on all the screens.
First, he welcomed the new Leader, thanked all other leaders for excepting his decision.
Ulae welcomed all the people on Earth, and wished them a great

future, a new beginning.
He made a promise to clear the Earth from the virus, if the Earths Leader agreed with his last wish.

Ulae was silent for a moment.
Then he began.

"MY LAST WISH FOR EARTH IS NOT DIFFICULT.
IT CAN BE DONE AND WILL TAKE TIME FOR ALL TO ADJUST TO THE NEW WAY OF LIFE.
OVER MANY, MANY YEARS, YOU HAVE KILLED, SLAUGHTERED, ARGUED OVER THE COLOUR OF YOUR SKIN, WITH NO RESPECT FOR EACH OTHER.
WITH NO RESPECT FOR LIFE.
YOUR DISBELIEVE IN WHAT EACH OF YOU HAVE TO OFFER.
YOUR TRUST IN EACH OTHER HAS BEEN POOR.
YOUR CHILDREN GROW WITH NO RESPECT FOR THEIR PARENTS,EACH OTHER OR THEIR FRIENDS.
GREED, POWER, AND POSSESSIONS ARE MORE IMPORTANT THAN FAMILIES.
THE NEED TO WORK HARDER, LONGER, TO PAY YOUR BILL, HAS BECOME YOUR LIFE.
FORGOTTEN ARE THE OLD ARTS, OLD CRAFTS, AND WAYS OF OLD.
YOUR CRUEL WAY OF LIVING HAS TAKEN AWAY THE LOVE, RESPECT AND TRUST DUE TO YOUR FAMILIES.
YOU SHOULD BE GOING FORWARD, INSTEAD YOU ARE GOING BACKWARDS.
YOUR TECHNOLOGY HAS MOVED AHEAD, BUT WITH THAT, MANY THINGS HAVE BEEN LOST.
YOUR CHILDREN LEARN VIOLENCE, WHICH MAKES UNDERSTANDING LOVE, HARD.
HATE, JEALOUSY, UNHAPPINESS, GREED, CRUELTY, HAVE ALL BECOME PART OF YOUR LIVES.

YOUR CHILDREN NEED TO BE GIVEN LOVE, UNDERSTANDING, AND RESPECT, TO LEARN TO RESPECT EACH OTHER.
THEY NEED TO RESPECT THE OLD, AND THEIR PARENTS, CARE FOR ANIMALS, AND YOUR WILDLIFE.
THEY NEED TO LEARN TO HOW TO GROW FOOD, HOW THE FOOD THEY EAT ENDS UP IN SHOPS, AND ON THEIR PLATE.
THEY NEED TO LEARN THAT WATER DOES NOT JUST COME OUT OF A TAP, THAT IT'S THE RAIN, THAT FILLS YOUR TANKS AND DAMS THAT MAKES IT A POSSIBILITY
THEY NEED TO KNOW THAT EVERY LIFE IS A GIFT, TO BE KIND TO ALL CREATURES, BIG AND SMALL.
BE KIND TO ALL PEOPLE WHATEVER THEIR COLOUR.
IT IS NOW UP TO YOU AS A RACE TO LEARN AGAIN TO LIVE TOGETHER.
NO MORE FIGHTING FOR POWER, GREED, AND GAIN.
YOU MUST WORK TOGETHER, LEARN FROM EACH OTHER, PUT BEHIND YOU YOUR
MISTAKES ENJOY THE GOOD THINGS YOU HAVE IN LIFE.
I HAVE CHOSEN YOUR LEADER; YOU WILL ALL LISTEN AND LEARN A NEW WAY OF LIFE.
IT WILL TAKE TIME FOR YOU TO ADJUST.
I WILL GO NOW, WITH ONE REQUEST THAT I ASK YOU FOR, FOR YOU ALL TO LIVE IN A WORLD OF PEACE AND HAPPINESS."

Ulae, after that speech, he ended his contact.
Ulae contacted the new world leader, with hope that everyone else had come to terms with his conditions.
All previous Leaders were still online; some paced the floor, not happy with what Ulae had asked from them.
Most were not happy that he chose Australia, but they had no more time to choose. And now, if they don't agree, life as they

knew it would be no more.
Ulae began with a welcoming speech.
And moved straight into the importance of his speech.

Ulae begans with a welcome speech,
And moves on to the importance of his speech.

'YOU HAVE NO TIME LEFT TO ARGUE, DISAGREE OR CHANGE YOUR MIND.
I HAVE GIVEN YOU THE CHOICE TO AGREE.
THOSE WHO CANNOT COME TO TERMS WITH THIS, WILL WILL NOT BE LEFT IN CHARGE, YOU WILL BEDISMISSED.
AUSTRALIA IS NOW YOUR RULER.
YOU NOW MUST ACCEPT THE RULES THAT I HAVE GIVEN YOU.
ACCEPT YOUR LEADER TO MAKE THIS WORK.
BUILT THE EMPIRE.
YOUR CHILDREN, NO MATTER THEIR COLOUR ARE YOUR FUTURE.
AS FROM TODAY, YOU HAVE THE CHANCE TO BUILD A NEW WORLD.
THE ONLY THING I AM ASKING FROM YOU IS PEACE.
FOR YOU TO WORK TOGETHER AS ONE.
NO MORE FIGHTING FOR POWER.
NO MORE WILL YOU SEE COLOUR AS A THREAT.
YOU MUST ALL BE AS ONE, LEARN TEACH EACH OTHER THAT NO MATTER WHAT COLOUR YOUR SKIN, YOU ARE THE SAME.
ONLY THEN, WILL I KNOW THAT YOUR WORLD HAS BEEN WORTH SAVING.
I NEED YOU NOW TO SEND ME YOUR ANSWER, EACH COUNTRY TO COME FARWARD TO AGREE TO WHAT I AM ASKING.
AS SOON AS YOU DO, THEN I CAN HELP YOU RID THE

EARTH FROM THE VIRUS.
YOU HAVE ONE EARTH HOUR TO DO THIS.
THEN I WILL HELP YOU.'

Leaders were not happy and argued over so many things. They seemed to forget that they only had one hour to agree.

CHAPTER 14

Meanwhile on planet Plasmator...
Amber was having a great time bonding with her mother,
Together they cooked, Amber trying many different foods that she had never tried before.
Also, she Explored the forests for new birds and animals.
Birds had colours, never seen on Earth.
Peacocks, the colours of the rainbow.
Pink ducks, golden doves.
Butterflies sparkle in the sunlight, fluorescent blues, pink, purple.
Unicorns galloped happily around her.
She feels she is in a dream.
The flowers so amazing growing wild, they too were bright and beautiful.
Fruit trees dripping with fruit, some she had never seen before.
Lakes and ponds full of ducks and swans.
Amber's mother took her too many places, to see many different animals, some she was familiar with. Others she had never seen before.

The people on Plasmator are friendly, happy and helpful.
Children play together happily, but know when it's time to help their parents or the elderly.
All on Plasmator wore bright colors, even the men wore bright clothing..
Plasmator is cheerful happy races that live as one in happiness.

When a new child is born to a family, they have a flower day.
Everyone brings flowers, the colors of rainbows, and of cause a

great feast is laid out on tables.
The new born are given a gift, anything from a jewel, something handmade or a toy.
Dance and music heard till late into the night.

Plasmator has no churches, instead they have harvest day every season.
Big halls are filled with jewels and filled with flowers, wheat, and hay bales.
Everyone brings what they have grown or made.
Bread, cheese, cakes, trays of vegetables and fruit.
A big fire pit in the middle of the hall is lit.
Music and dance fills the hall with laughter and song.
At the end of the night, everyone helps themselves to what they can carry home.

They don't eat much red meat on Plasmator. mostly chicken.
But do eat lots of eggs, drink milk, and eat fish.
Any animal that dies of old age or injury are feed to the meat- eating animals, like lions and tigers.
Dogs and cats eat fish, eggs and vegetables.
With only one cat and dog for each family.
Horses roam free, goats and cows in fields, sheep and chickens are also free to roam were ever they please in the fields.

The weather is much the same as Earths, wind, rain, snow in winter, but their summers are never as hot as Earths.
All the meat eaters have a big island of their own, surrounded by a mass of water.
Each island for certain species.
Different environments, like on Earth.

You can take a tour on a hovercraft, little car like buses that hover over the land.
As they do not have cars only hover crafts, small bug- like vehicles.

No semis or trucks only bigger hover bugs.
No planes or helicopters all hover craft, easy to drive as you only have to push a button to where you want to go, and it does it for you, which is quite amazing.
If you want to go to the other side of the planet, just step inside the travel bug it's a bit like a telephone box, push a button and you are there in moments most of the hard work is done by robots, so is most of the boring work.

CHAPTER 15

Down on Earth there is still chaos, no one sure what would happen next.
Blacks and whites were now disagreeing with each other, and no one obeying the police any more.,
People were .still killing each other
Riots, rallies, destruction continued.
Could what Ulae wanted, be asking be too much? Will it work?
China didn't want to get on with the rest of the world.
Grown, sophisticated men, in need of power.
They weren't happy with the promise of a new way of life'
The Earth was a mess.
Ulae shook his head, he wondered, should he help them or just destroy them.
Ulae needed to tell them something else, something that might help them.
So once again he took over the Leaders airways. What they hear shocks them.

"A LEADER THAT YOU HAD MANY YEARS AGO, HAD A SON THAT YOU ALL THOUGHT HAD DIED IN A PLANE CRASH.
THIS SON IS ALIVE AND WELL.
HE HAS BEEN ON MY PLANET PLASMATOR LEARNING OUR WAY OF LIFE.
HE IS NOW BACK ON EARTH TO HELP AND SHOW YOU THE RIGHT WAY.
HE DID NOT THINK AMERICA WAS THE ONE TO RULE, HE IS NOW ON EARTH AND WILLING TO SHOW THE

WAY.
IT IS HE WHO HELPED MAKE THE DECISION TO CHOOSE AUSTRALIA.
YOU WILL BE INFORMED SHORTLY.
HE WILL BECOME YOUR AUSTRALIAN INFORMER.
YOUR TIME IS RUNNING OUT.YOU HAVE 30 MINUTES TO AGREE WITH MY WISH."

And then he is gone again, leaving the Leaders once again in shock
But with the short time they had, it was now time to put up an agreement
.Slowly the Leaders on Earth entered into the plan. They were uneasy.
They hoped for good news of how to rid the world of the virus.
Not to come to some agreement.
What will it be, the missile or, the help from Ulae?
One by one all agreeing and sighing the pledge
As the clock ticks closer to doomsday, everyone's nerves were on edge.
The virus still crept across the globe. still killing anything and everything in its path .
No one knew if an agreement had been made.
A strange form of silence was felt across the Earth.
Mother's hugged their children, and together sat without saying a word, waiting in hope.
Not a car on the roads, as everyone was inside waiting.
Many wept in silence.
Strong men, tears ran down their faces, they hugged their wives or partners.

As the doomsday clock struck 12, they waited, knowing this could be the end.
With that, China decided to let off a nuclear missile, the button was pushed.

The missile reached the target, to rid the virus.
The news of this reached the other leaders on Earth.
WHY? Did they do that? Who gave them the order to fire the missile?
Tempers rose, voices loud and angry.
China's response:"Ulae has not done what we asked, we need to know if the missiles will work."
We cannot wait in hope he will be back to help, we have waited long enough."
All other Leaders were in shock and not sure what to do.
The nuclear missile's smoke could be seen as a big mushroom on all satellites.
Destruction swept across the land.
Everything was wiped out, for miles around.

The Australian Leader was not happy, as it was up to him to make the decision.
All Leaders's immediately tried to contact Ulae.

Suddenly, without any warning, like lightning strikes, big objects appeared in the skies, blue, green and purple.
They hovered over all cities on Earth.
A song of horns droned over all cities.
They sat in the sky, bigger then football fields, flashing, blue white.
Laser lights flashed down, in fluorescent green and blue white.
They hovered for 10 minutes, before Ulae took over all airways.

As the doomsday clock strikes 12 they wait, knowing this could be the end.

"YOU HAVE DONE NOW WHAT WE MAY NOT BE ABLE TO STOP.
YOU ALL AGREED TO THE NEW WAY OF LIFE.
AND NOW YOU DO THIS.
I NEED TO TALK TO FRANK BEFOR I CAN HELP YOU.

PLEASE WALK HIM OUT NOW."
With that he was gone.

Frank was led outside. he waited a moment ,then a beam of light surrounded him, The next thing he knew, he was in one of the hovering crafts next to Ulae.

Ulae greeted him with a handshake, Amber appeared from the next room, and they embraced.
Frank and Amber, so happy and overjoyed to see each other, hug and kiss, Ulae broke them apart.
"We have work to do! Ulae's voice stern and firm.
'I don't know now if I can help your planet, they have no respect for the planet',
Ulae was angry and upset.
"I asked them not to use their weapons, they disobeyed my orders..
I cannot trust them now."

Franks stood and looked around, still overwhelmed by being beamed up.
Amber is trying to tell him about her time on Plasmator, but his not able to take it all in.
Ulaes on the speakers abusing the leaders on Earth
"YOU COULD NOT WAIT; I HAVE NO CHOICE NOW, AS I CAN NOT NOW HELP YOU."
The whole experience was too much to take in; Frank found a seat and sat down.
Frank finds his voice, "What happens now?" he asked Ulae.

Ulae turned to Frank, he did not smile. .
His words shocked both Frank and Amber.
"I am sorry, but I may not be able to help your people now.
I have told them not to use the nuclear weapons, but they have."

Amber was removed from the control room.

An hour later, things on Earth became complicated, countries now fought each other, and weapons were used to destroy each other.
Frank had his say," Its only one country that has done this".
Ulae hit another button, 'Open your eyes Frank, see those mush-roomed bellows of smoke? They are not fires they are from war weapons".

"Have they gone mad'? Frank asked. He stood looking at the Earth, in shock...
Ulae,replied,
"Yes! But now the virus will not be able to be stopped".
"Why not? Frank questioned.

Ulae looked at Frank his eyes showed sadness.
"The planet Earth, will now, not be able to be helped.
They did not listen to what I had explained.
And now I have to do what I have done before."

"And what might that be?" Frank asked Ulae.
Ulae sighed, he walked around the room,
"I am sorry but I have to do this have done it many times before".
"Done what?" Frank wanted to know..
Ulae looked out the big window, at the Earth.

He turned to Frank,"Why do you think I asked for you to come with me?"
Frank shook his head, 'I don't know, tell me."
Ulae turned to Frank and puts his arm around franks shoulder.
"I love my daughter...., she loves you, if I didn't take you off your planet, and Amber would never have forgiven me.
Your horses and dog are here, you have no family on Earth, so you won't miss them."

Ulae.I does have friends that I care about and love",
I am sorry about that Frank."

'What I must do now, you may not forgive me for, but it must be done.
I have had to do this many times before, I do not like to do this, but after giving your planet Earth so many chances, the time has now come to destroy them".

Franks ears cannot believe what he is hearing.
"You cannot be serious! You cannot destroy everyone on Earth, that's insane," Frank splattered.

Ulae replied.
"Egypt was a great intelligent race, but they too wanted power, had slaves, and only cared for themselves, Kings and queens, in big building, built by slaves.
Their people were poor, starving, and lived in poverty.
Only the kings and queens had the best, they treated their people badly.

They took whatever they wanted.'
Many countries are now the same.

China wants to gain power gain power, buying up property, land, and moving in to take over the Earth.
They are a cruel race, they cut the legs off the cattle and dogs so to make it easy to skin them alive ,or blowtorch them ,then throw them into boiling pots while still alive, they have no pity.
Yes, they need food but to be cruel is not the way.
They skin the cows while they are still alive.
I could say more, but that race must go.
That is only one country of many that have become cruel.
Argentina and Uruguay bleed mares at 40 weeks in foal for their plasma, they take 10 liters of blood each time, they abort the foals, and these are blood farms .they sell the blood for millions of dollars to stock breeders to improve their stock. 25 mares die each day as they take too much blood for greed .the rests are left weak.
I could go on but that race also has to go.

That is only one of many that have become cruel and have lost the reason they live.
Many countries are now at war over things that are trivial".

Frank was silent, he could not take in what Ulae was about to do.

As they stood staring out the big window to Earth, another mushroom cloud was seen.
North Korea had let off two missiles towards America.
And with that, America had sent missiles back at them.

Jets on Earth screamed through the skies.
Warships and submarines were having battles, at sea.

Ulae told Frank that there was not much he could do; they are at war with each other to become the superpower.
So, Ulae informed Frank that it was time to stop the fighting.

"Frank, this is not something I like to do.
That's another reason I choose Australia to rule.
They will not be too affected.
The missile they dropped was dropped in the outback outback.
It will be a while before they can use that land again.
But the rest of the country will be fine as soon as I give the order to my troops.
First, I must talk to the new leader in Australia".

CHAPTER 16

Ulae hit a button and broke into the computer were the Australian leader was seated.
The Australian leader worried, unsure, as now the Earth was at war.
Ulae waits a moment.

"DO I HAVE YOUR ATTINTION?" Ulae waits a moment....
He waited for an answer.
"Yes we are hearing you loud and clear",
The Australian leader came forward to speak.

"I am sorry, but the world is at war, no one wants to give up their power.
Can you still help us?"
Ulae can now only tell them what he had to do.

"I AM SORRY TO HAVE TO TELL YOU THIS.
BUT THERE IS NOTHING LEFT FOR ME TO DO.
I CAN'T HELP THEM NOW.
IT IS NOW UP TO YOU.
TO BUILT A EMPIE,
AUSTRALIA STILL HAS A CHANCE TO MAKE IT WORK.
LIKE I SAID YOU HAVE ONE DECADE TO DO THIS.
IF NOT, I WILL DESTROY YOU.
AUSTRALIA IS A BIG YOUNG COUNTRY.
YOU HAVE PEOPLE FROM ALL NATIONS.
YOU MUST LEARN TO LIVE TOGEATHER.
WORK AS ONE, NO MATTER WHAT COULOR YOUR

SKIN.
NEWZEALAND, TASMANIA, AND THE SMALL ISLANDS THAT SURROUNDS YOUR COUNTRY CAN BE SPARED.
THE REST OF THE WORLD WILL HAVE TO BE ERASED.
I AM NOT A CRUEL MAN, THIS IS NOT WHAT I LIKE TO DO.
I HAVE HAD TO DO THIS MANY TIMES.
BE THANKFUL YOU HAVE BEEN SPARED.
I COULD HAVE HELPED THEM, BUT NOW IT'S TOO LATE.
THEY HAVE USED THE NUCLEAR WEAPONS.
MY CRAFTS ARE ABOVE YOUR CITIES, WAITING FOR MY COMMAND
IS THERE ANYTHING YOU WOULD LIKE TO SAY BEFORE I LEAVE?"

The Australian leader was speechless for a moment.
I—I don't know what to say? I need some time to think this over. You cannot destroy the innocent people, can we talk about this some more?"
Ulae give his apology and told him, there is no more time,
YOU WILL NOT BE ABLE TO LEAVE YOU COUNTRY FOR AT LEST 7 EARTH YEARS AS IT WILL BE CONTAMINATED AND THAT WOULD KILL YOU.
I SHALL TALK WITH YOU ONCE THIS IS OVER".

With that he stopped conversing with the Australian leader, who now was devastated.

CHAPTER 17

The Australian leader now in panic, he ordered all jets, ships and submarines to head home.
What should I tell the people? Should I say anything? He is not sure what to do.
Some Australian people had family overseas, what should he say?

He calls all his politicians to a meeting.
Slowly they filed in, those who could not make the meeting waited on line, computers at the ready.
When all were settled, he began the meeting.
Not knowing how to start or what he should say, he mumbled,

"Thank you for your attendance."
"Ulae has informed me that he cannot help us.
Now that war has broken out in many countries.
With nuclear weapons being used, the virus will spread across the world.
The people on Earth will not be able to fight this.
They will die a miserable painful death.
If not from war, they'll die from the virus.
With food shortage and no one working the people will panic."
They will starve to death, in their own homes if they still have one.
There will be nothing left for them to live for.
Ulae has informed me that he has no other option now.
He has said this has been done many times here on Earth.
And is now time to do this once again.
Ulae has no joy having to do this, but knows now, that it is time.

All history that we know of, and history that has been a mystery, has now been explained.
Lost cities, Atlanta, The mystery behind Egypt's tombs and pyramids.
Dinosaurs of all kinds.
The reasonable explanation of Aliens now answered..
There is life beyond this planet...
We know that now.
He came from a planet far from ours to help us.
We let him down.
All of us to blame, we have become a violent, cruel race.
Forgetting that life is a gift.
Too caught up with what we want and we can have.
Ulae is right, family has lost the love, the feeling of giving, helping each other.
He was asking nothing from us but peace, happiness, and to love each other no matter what our colour.
Ulae has said this is the longest that the Earth has had, to come to peace with each other.
Australia has been chosen to make things right.
We will be the only ones left to do this.
We have been given one decade to do this, or we to will be destroyed.
It is up to us now, to work together, with no war or fighting.
Build the empire he has ask for, learn the new ways that he wants".

A son of a leader that we once thought dead has been with Ulae learning his way.
He will be here soon, to help us get through this.

Ulae will soon be back to rid Australia of the virus.
The rest of the world will be destroyed."

All in the room mumbled, they talked and were shocked by what they had just been told.
Questions had to be answered.

What will we be telling the people?
Will we be able to stop Ulae doing this?
What about our family's who live elsewhere?
How will this be done?
Will anyone survive?
Should we warn the rest of the world, tell them what was about to happen?

"Ulae has asked me to say nothing as it will cause panic, and unnecessary sadness.
If you try to make a call to loved ones your call will be blocked.
Be thankful you and your family have been spared.
No one is to leave this building, all that are listening on line to stay where you are, and have no contact with anyone ,until the deed has been done'.

"Ulae has promised it will not be painful, how he will do this I have no idea".
The Australian leader began to read from the silver file that Ulae has given him.
The exploitation of what Ulae expected from them.
When all has been said, and questioning answered.
They are sat down to enjoy, if they could, a meal and wine.
As they talked, they brought up many "if's and maybes'.
They had a hard time coming to terms with what had to be done.

Ulae comes in over the Australian government computers again.

"MY TROOPS WILL DESTROY THE VIRUS FOR YOU IN 10 EARTH MINUTES.
PLEASE STAY IN YOUR HOMES UNTILL WE HAVE SUCCEEDED.

I WILL INFORM YOU WHEN THIS HAS BEEN DONE".
The announcement was sent to all Australians.
People stopped what they were doing and gathered around their computers, and televisions.
They waited to see what would happen next.

10 minutes later a sound of thunder, the roar of a freight train was heard.
The sky filled with enormous giant spheres, flashes of light filled the skies.
The sky went dark, as they hovered over the cities in Australia.
There lights flashing the colours of the rainbow.
The horns are blown, so loud it make you shiver.
People ran inside their homes to hide, others go outside to see what was going on.
Children cried with fear.
Then there is silence.

Minutes later Ulae's voice was heard loudly across the country.

"PLEASE GO BACK TO YOUR HOMES, STAY INSIDE.
WE ARE HERE TO RID YOU OF THE VIRUS.
A MIST WILL FILL THE SKY, PLEASE DO NOT BE ALARMED.
THERE WILL BE A LOT OF NOISE AND LIGHT, DO NOT BE AFRAID.
THIS WILL TAKE 20 EARTH MINUTES"

People began to rush back inside their homes, and they waited.

Outside, the noise picked up.
Lights flashed like lightning throughout the skies.
And then a strange blue-white mist drifted through, like fog.
It drifted between buildings, through the trees and landscape, .a eerie silent fog, with no smell or taste.

20 minutes later there was silence.
The fog fades away.

No one was game to go outside.
They all waited.. . it was over.
Ulae informed the Australian leader, that they were finally free of the virus.
Ulae asked them to wait 30 minutes before going outside.
Everyone in the room, that have been standing in front of the computers, cheered with joy.
After the excitement of hearing the good news, the cheering died down.

The Australian leader informs all Australians that the threat of the virus is now over for them.
He does not tell them the horrid news just yet, that the rest of the world was about to be destroyed.
The Australian leader was pulled aside, a urgent voice asked him to come with him, as something has come up that he needed to attend to.
As he walked towards the door he was greeted by someone, The American Leaders son that ever one believed had died, years ago.
The Australian leader broke out into a sweat, the shock, overwhelmed him.
They shook hands.
He introduce himself, and he followed the Australian leader, he was given a seat in front of all the politicians that were there.
All were amazed, overwhelmed, they could not believe who had just entered the room.
All in the room were silent.
The Australian Leader gives him the nod to speak.

"Ulae has sent me here to show you the way, guide you through the new way of life.
I have spent many years on Plasmator, learning Ulae's way.

It may take some time for you to adjust to his way of life, but believe me it can work.
I am here to help your leader with all he needs to know.
We will build the empire Ulae has asked you to build.

We will teach the young, to be grateful for everything that they have and been given.
The colour of a person's skin, will, never be used as different.
All will be the same, no more will they fight over colour,race or for greed.
The gifts that the Earth has to offer will be recognized.
The young will learn to respect all life on Earth.
They will learn to be respectful, to look after their elders, and respect their parents.
A new way of learning will begin.
Ulae will replenish the Earth in a decade; the world will begin again in a new and peaceful way,
Ulae will bring back the wildlife, once the forests have grown back.
We must not go beyond our boundaries before it's time.

Ulae, has said we must work on building our world here, before we do more.
All counties will be given their wildlife back as was before .after the decade.
But we must respect and learn from this.
No more hunting, killing for gain or fun.

No more will you cut down the forests, and bulldoze the environment.
Gold and diamonds will have no great value.
Money will be worthless, people will work for what they need, or want,
Helping, giving, and caring will be the way of life to live.
Factories will still be needed, but must give to the community,

make a living, with no great gain.
Wildlife should be treated with respect, their environment cared for.
You all and I have been given the chance to make this work.

Meanwhile Frank, still floating in a craft in the universe, was unsure what Ulae had in mind.
Frank is pacing the floor, He can see that all hell had broken lose on Earth."I need to see Amber' he shouts to Ulae.
"She is fine, look here."He hits a button and shows Amber, outside in the field picking flowers with her mother, smiling, and with their dog Hades.
"You will be together soon," Ulae informs Frank.
"What are you going to do?" asks Frank.
"What I should have done years ago", replies Ulae.
"What I told you I must do Frank!
"You can't do it, please rethink this?" Frank begs Ulae.
Ulae does not answer.
He has become tried of repeating to Frank what has to be done.
He walks away, leaving Frank standing alone looking out the big window down at Earth.

Ulae, in another room was trying to come to terms now that he has to do something he never likes to do.
He knows it has to be done, and the time is now, but to doing it, he knows will break the hearts of Amber and Frank.
Ulae goes back to the computer room."Follow me Frank', I will lead you to Amber, she can show you around Plasmator".

Frank follows Ulae to a small craft; Frank was welcomed by a lady. She smiles and tells Frank she will take him to be with Amber!
Ulae watches on a screen as Frank and Amber are united.
The screens of Earth are now what he must focus on.
He looks at the screens and asks forgiveness, for what he now has to do.

He contacts his troops, who are patiently waiting in their crafts ready for Ulae's word to go. .

Down on Earth the big hover crafts that have been hovering over the cities blow their horns .beams of light stream from them down to Earth.
The people on Earth have been waiting inside there homes, hoping that Ulae is about to help them.
The Leaders were waiting and watching their computers and screens, hoping all to go well.
But what was about to happen was definitely not what they were expecting!

CHAPTER 18

Ulae his eyes full with tears, knowing when he gives the command, there will be no coming back from it.
Ulae gives his troops the command.
All troops go into action, the skies fill with the loud sound of horns, the roar of war crafts, and laser lights of all colours.

A fluorescent Green mist, drifts over the Earth, creeping through cracks and windows.
Animals lie down and sleep. Birds fall from the trees, Children and babies, pets, within a hour all were sleeping.

Silence was everywhere, The mist fades slowly and disappears.,
The crafts have left. Shooting once again into the heavens.
The Earth was sleeping, not a sound to be heard.
But no one will wake up from this,
Every man women and child, every living thing now in a deep sleep
Never again will they wake.

Millions of people in a deep sleep, the world a silent place.
Left now to rot decay, Those in bunkers thinking to be safe also in a deep sleep.
Once again as before the Earth was destroyed.

But this time Australia and the surrounding Islands have been given the chance to begin again.

Ulae informs Australia that the deed had been done.
Australian citizens are wondering, why, they cannot get on any

oversea computer sights?

Why they cannot call their loved ones overseas?
Wondering? Why, their phones do not work?

The now Ruler of the Earth, the Australian Leader, has to explain and tell the nation the news that would be hard for all to come to terms with.
There was no easy way to do this.
All politicians in Australia unsure how to go about it..
After hours of talk, coming to terms that there is no more than them on the Planet.
They know they must tell the Australian people the disturbing news.
With all news channels, now having breaking news, of no contact with anyone overseas and wondering why their news crews are not contacting them.
The now Ruler, had to go on air and tell the nation the horrid news.
Before the Ruler went on air, he tells all news stations to ask all citizens to listen to his speech, to be in 30 minutes.
This runs across all screens for that next 30 minutes.
With all waiting sitting in front of there televisions and computers, again they waited.

The Ruler went straight to the point of his speech.

"As from now I will be your Leader.
What I say from now on will be the law.
If you do not approve of my law you will be dealt with.
We are to embark on a new way of life.
No more will the Colour of your skin you religion be a sin
From this day on every person will be treated the same.
Any fighting over colour or race must end today.
Anyone who has a problem with this will be arrested and dealt

with.
And now, I must tell you all that yes, we have been rid of the virus.

But it has come with a sacrifice.
Ulae has spared us, Australia, to renew the world.
I know the reason why you have no internet connection from overseas.
What, I am about to explain to you now, will shock you, will make you fill angry and upset.
But you must come to terms with it.
You will feel grief, sadness, and pain; you may not be able to come to understand for some time.
But it had been done.

Ulae has done this many times before.
It is not something he likes to do.
But the time came, and Ulae made the decision to do it.
With the world unsettled, at war, cruelty, hate, and fighting over colour and race.
We have been spared, but unfortunately the rest of the world, every man women and child has been destroyed.
No more, will you be able to contact your loved ones, We are all that has been left to start a peaceful world.
All animals every living thing, everything has been destroyed.
What I can tell you, Ulae has said it was peaceful without pain.
I will leave now so you can come to terms with this.

In tears, fear, shock and disbelief, people cannot believe what they have just been told.
Anger, hate and pain, takes over.
With all in shock, they are left to go through a lot of upset and pain.
The politicians cannot help them in their unhappiness, sadness.
All Australians left in shock, crying for loved ones now lost.

The Australian citizens left to experience something they have never had to experience ever before.
The thought of being the only ones left on the planet Earth takes some time to take in.
But knowing they have been spared, and given the chance to make change slowly over time began to show.

One month later the Ruler talks to the people. His words are simple and caring.
He begins with how he knows the lose to be great, very hard to except.
But now he says it is time to move on.

We must show Ulae we can do this.
Together we will build the Empire.
No more will we fight, be cruel, hurt or maim.
We will work together as one.
Ulae's rules will take time to adjust to, we are Australians we can do this.
As the people began to adjust to the new way of life ,except that it is up to them to make it work ,they look at every sunrise as a blessing..

Meanwhile on Plasmator Frank and Amber have been informed of the destruction of Earth, and been told that Australia has been spared.
They are told that the Leader once thought dead is there to help, as he knows the rules and ways to be expected.
In one decade they will be able to watch as the wildlife is returned to every forest.
To watch as life on Earth begins again.

This story will be continued, in one decade.
Story by Linda Lorraine.

This one!

THE END

Poems
by
Linda Lorraine

TO ALL THE CHILDREN

To all the little children
All those yet not born
Let's learn to live together
Learn to be as one
No matter what your colour
No matter what your race
Inside we are all the same
Our dreams, our goals and place
A new world is beginning
Let's help to make it right

Believe in each other
Let's try to do this right
Everything that has been done
It's now up to you
It's your world go and live it
The fun is for you
Do it with no fighting, for money or for greed
All way's look behind you to see what you achieved
Remember we are all the same
Live your life, your dream

A NEW BEGINING

As I sit by my window
Look out at the trees
I think of all the wildlife
That, depend on these
Last year, the grass was brown
This year so green

The kangaroo's are grazing
Joey's by their side
Some of them are playing
Others like to hide

Kookaburras Laughing
High up in the tree's
Magpies are all singing songs
So hard to believe

Wood ducks are all happy
Swimming in the pond
No water last year, without that they were gone
Butterflies are dancing
Blown in by the breeze
Always makes you wonder
In drought, how, did they breed
All little creatures have babies by their side
None of them now stressing, for water they must find

THE PEACOCK

The colours of a rainbow,

A blue crown on his head,

Across his head the deepest blue,

Runs down to his chest,

His colours sparkle in the sun,

All greens, blues and gold.

His tail is now shimmering,

He is putting on a show,

The girls just stop and look at him,

As he dances in the breeze,

So many eyes stare back at them,

As he shimmers more to please.

A bright white strip across his eyes,

He looks so much at ease,

How wonderful is nature,

To give colour that's so bright,

You only know, when you see one,

That God did this one right.

JOEY

A mother kangaroo with Joey,

Makes a big mistake,

To jump before a car she does, She dies, So sad.

She leaves a bub behind.

No milk, no warmth, no mum no more.

I take the little Joey,I hold her by my side,

I give her milk and love,

She grows with me, in a cloth pouch she does hide.

Twelve months it takes to raise her,

My trust she lives to learn,

Never will I leave her, her new journey has begun.

A second chance, she has been given,

To go back in the wild,

She will never forget me, I'm her mum she knows I am wise,

It is sad to see her go, but I know it has to be,,

I know she will come back to me, if sick or in need

Now she has a Joey of her own, she shows it off to me,

I tell her I am proud of her, for all that it is worth,

She can always come back to me whenever she does please...

www.ingramcontent.com/pod-product-compliance
Lightning Source LLC
LaVergne TN
LVHW040155080526
838202LV00042B/3166